The Innocent Outlaw

By
Mike Dale

Trent Conway

Table of Contents

Chapter One

"Which way did he go?" Trent Conway heard the marshal roar.

"He rode that way. After him!" the sheriff cried.

"Is that him? On the grey horse?" the marshal queried.

"Yes, that's him alright," the sheriff replied. "Get him and make him bleed for his crime!"

Trent could feel his throat constrict. He could, in fact, feel the noose around his neck—and it was tightening. He began to choke, his hand flying up to his throat to release the bands that had cut off his air supply. He writhed in agony, his body twisting this way and that. He tried to grasp the noose and wrench it off his throat, but he couldn't.

"Get him!" the sheriff was shouting. "Get the varmint!"

Shots rang out in the night. He could hear loud wails of anguish.

Trent doubled up, took a ragged breath, and tore the bands off his throat. He sat up gasping for air and looked around, grateful that his pursuers hadn't snared him when he had passed out.

It had happened a few times along the way, the flashbacks, and they were relentless and realistic, playing out the scene that had taken place only hours ago. He was alone now, more alone than ever before, with not a soul who would clear his name. He knew nobody believed in his innocence. Not even his Aunt Mary. She had always been on his side, but even she had suddenly turned against him.

"Get out, Trent!" He could hear her shrill scream even now, as he climbed onto Eagle. "How could you do it? How could you even think you would get away with it? Oh, that beautiful girl. You didn't deserve her, and look what you've done!"

"Aunt Mary," Trent had cried, "please listen to me. This is a setup. I never did it. How could you even think that I would do something so… so… sinful?"

"Leave this minute, Trent. Go! Just go! I can't even bear to look at you!"

Trent Conway had got shakily to his feet and stumbled to his grey horse. Eagle seemed unphased by the recent gunfight, and faithfully carried his master to safety.

"We've gotta get going again, Eagle, my friend," Trent gasped, reaching for the canteen that hung from the horse's saddle and taking a large slug of water from it.

"The next town we're at, Eagle, I'll get you a carrot. Oh yes, I'll get you several carrots. You're a good boy, Eagle. You sure saved my life today," Trent murmured, his mouth set in a thin hard line as he remembered the bullets coming at him. But no gunfire could match the words that came at him from his Aunt Mary, the same woman who had taken care of him after his mother had left and gone her way.

"All I ask is shelter for one night, and I'll be on my way in the morning, Aunt Mary," Trent had pleaded, holding up his bleeding arm.

"You go rot in hell, Trent. I didn't raise you like my own for you to pay me back like this. Oh no, I didn't."

"I didn't do it, Aunt Mary, you have to believe me," Trent repeated.

"And I didn't raise you to be a liar, Trent Conway, so my door is closed to you. Now go! And remember, I might spare your life, but the Good Lord above will judge you for what you did. You will pay, boy, you will pay!"

Trent drove his spurs determinedly into Eagle's side, and the horse flew across the rolling plains, taking him further and further away from Woodson County. Even as he covered the miles, Trent became increasingly aware that he was embarking on the life of a fugitive, and all for one mistake that he had made.

"A love crime, they're calling it, Trent… a love crime! What does that even mean? How could someone who loved someone else do what you did and then ask for refuge?"

"Aunt Mary, could you let me explain please?" Trent had cried in frustration. "Please, just listen to my side of the story!"

"I can't hear one more word about this, Trent, not another word! I don't want to be associated with a… with someone… like you!" his aunt had screamed.

"I'll go. Just stop yelling at me, Aunt Mary, and I'll go," Trent had murmured. "I just need something to bind my wound and stop the blood."

"You're worried about stopping your blood, are you, Trent?" his aunt had ground out through clenched teeth. "Well, I'm not. I'm more worried about innocent blood…"

Trent's memories were interrupted by the sound of approaching horses, and he jumped on Eagle, galloping faster as shots rang out. He was dodging bullets when he decided that he wasn't going to take the fire without fighting back. Only criminals ran like scared animals, and he was tired of running.

With a yell, he whipped about as Eagle galloped forward, and began to fire back at the men pursuing him. He couldn't see them, but it seemed like a lot of men to be going after just one person.

"Keep going, boy," Trent said to his horse, firing with both guns even as Eagle picked up the pace. He shifted position again, so that he was facing forward, and drove his spurs into Eagle's flank to point the horse in a different direction. After a while, the thunder of horses' hooves abated, and Trent Conway found himself galloping ahead alone.

He rode away without looking back, stopping along the way by a lake. He was oblivious to its beauty, and only aware of how elevated his heartbeat was as he lowered his arm into the water and watched the crystal clear surface turn a muddy shade of red. He sat back on his heels and tore his bandana off his neck, binding it firmly over the wound. He had hurriedly packed a few things in his saddlebag, and now he pulled out his buckskin jacket and threw it on, so that his wounded arm was well concealed. As he started to climb back onto Eagle, he saw a group of riders in the distance, coming towards him. Trent felt the hairs on the back of his neck bristle.

"Let's go, boy," he said to Eagle, spurring him into a gallop and trying hard not to look back.

As he rode, Trent realized he would have to disguise himself, no matter where he went. "There'll be *wanted* posters up all the way from Woodson County to Wichita by now, boy," he whispered to his horse. "So sorry, but we both are going to need new names, Eagle. And we'll stop at the first town that has a saloon. I need to bathe my wound with some whiskey if I want to avoid losing it."

Eagle whinnied as he galloped faster.

Chapter Two

Trent winced as the pain in his arm grew more pronounced and less bearable. The streets were dark as he rode into the dusty town. It looked decaying and down at the heel, and nothing about it served to elevate Trent's flagging spirits. Even its name, White Water, seemed incongruous and completely inappropriate. He would need a medic for sure, Trent thought to himself.

He slipped into the Lone Mustang Saloon, shoulders hunched and eyes down. He was trying his best not to look like the fugitive that he was, but his spirit was broken. For a moment, he wondered if it might just be best to let the so-called law have its way.

"You look like you've had a long ride," the bartender said, taking in Trent's disheveled appearance.

"I need a place to stay," Trent said, ignoring the bartender's remark. "And a bottle of whiskey."

"You can get a bottle of whiskey here and head to a room upstairs," the bartender said, eyeing Trent keenly as he handed him a key. "But if you want to eat, you'll have to come down here. Don't want no rats after chicken bones and leftover pieces of biscuit in your room."

Trent nodded, steeling himself for the next question.

"What's your name? Need to be sure who we're letting our rooms to and all. No offense meant, of course," the bartender remarked.

"Luke Grey," Trent said, without a moment's hesitation.

The bartender nodded and tipped his hat, and Trent escaped to the room he was directed to, carrying an oil lamp and his saddlebag.

In the room, Trent tore off his jacket and shirt and sloughed off the blood from his arm, inspecting his wound in the inadequate mirror. He poured a liberal quantity of whiskey on the wound and took several gulps himself. Sometime later, he shrugged his jacket on again, wincing at the pain in his arm, and went down into the saloon.

"You have a good medic here in these parts?" Trent asked the bartender, as the latter set a plate of food down in front of him.

"Depends what you want one for," the bartender replied, giving Trent a searching look. "You been in some kind of trouble?"

Trent shook his head, not feeling the need to share his story with this talkative stranger. "No. I need something for a fever I've been running for a few days."

"You'll have to wait until tomorrow," the bartender replied. "There's a doctor with a clinic across the street. He'll take care of you."

"Much obliged," Trent murmured, tipping his hat. He hurriedly spooned the plate of beans and potatoes down, aware that the bartender was watching his every move.

"How did you get shot?" the doctor asked the next day.

"I was set upon by bandits on the trail," Trent replied stoically. "Is the wound bad?"

"You'll live," the doctor replied with a hollow laugh. "You got alcohol on it well in time." He looked at Trent through narrowed eyes. "Where are you headed?"

Trent shrugged. "Right here, to White Water," he replied.

"Strange place to want to visit. You got business interests here?" the doctor asked.

Trent replied with an ironic laugh. "Business interests? No. I came in search of work," he said.

"Where have you come from?" the doctor asked.

Trent opened his mouth to reply with a well-rehearsed lie, when the door to the tiny clinic flew open and a man dropped to the floor bleeding.

"What, you again?" the doctor queried with a derisive snort. "What's your story this time?"

Trent took the opportunity to slip out of the clinic and went back to the saloon.

"Doctor fix you up?" the bartender asked.

Trent gave him a sharp look. "Well, I just needed some medication, not fixing up. And yes, I got what I needed, thank you. You wouldn't happen to know of any jobs going in these parts, would you?" he added.

"Depends on what you're good at. What kind of experience do you have?" the bartender asked.

"Regular ranch stuff," Trent answered, his thoughts flying back to Woodson County and his life there working on his father's ranch.

"Lots of ranches in White Water. Some distance from town, but they're there, and you can find work, I'm sure," the bartender said.

Trent nodded. "A man came into the doctor's clinic bleeding and almost passed out. The doctor seemed to imply that it wasn't the first time. Anything I should know about this town? Lots of violence here, perhaps? Or in the vicinity?" Trent asked.

"Maybe you shouldn't ask too many questions, Luke Grey," the bartender replied. "White Water has its secrets, same as any other town like this one. Things happen. We don't get involved. We go about our business. You want work? You get a job and you ask no questions. You just do what you're told and you get your pay. Try not to get above yourself and never get your nose in anyone else's business."

Trent took in this earful with a growing sense of apprehension.

The bartender leaned over the counter. "You know, Luke Grey, here's another piece of advice. If you're thinking you should ride on to the next town and find work there, you'll be riding a long time. Best to take what you're getting here."

"Hmm… I'll weigh my options," Trent murmured, regretting the words the moment they were out.

"Ha! Options!" the bartender snorted. "What options does a cowboy have but to work on a ranch? Any ranch. The weather'll be changing soon, you know, and it's never good to be on the trail in winter. But, of course, you know that. If I were you, I would get a job, stick to it, and earn enough to set up my own ranch."

"Sounds like you have it all figured out," Trent replied with a humorless laugh.

"Just a word of advice, that's all," the bartender replied.

"What's going on?" Trent asked suddenly, as the sound of gunshots filled the air outside.

"Just another day in White Water," the bartender shrugged. "Someone owes someone else money. Someone double-crosses someone else. Someone stole somebody's girl… all causes for a good old fashioned gunfight," he replied.

"You don't seem in the least disturbed by what's happening outside," Trent commented. "Aren't you afraid it'll be bad for business?"

"Oh, no. It's good for business," the bartender answered. "Fellas will shoot at each other, the Doc will fix them all up, and then they'll come in here for a drink, seated at opposite tables and glowering at each other, each ordering more whiskeys to get one up on the other."

"I see," Trent replied with a sigh. "It all seems quite straightforward, then?"

"Who said anything about straightforward?" the bartender said. "I'm just talking about life in White Water. Nothing straightforward about it. But we just carry right on."

"So, you got the word on any jobs, then?" Trent asked. He had to wait for the bartender to reply, because some customers came in just then and ordered drinks. That gave Trent some time to sit and ponder his situation over a glass of whiskey and a plate of beans.

After a while, the bartender came back over and picked up the conversation. "There's Rock Creek Ranch about three miles east of here. I know they're looking for a ranch hand, because theirs got wounded in a gunfight. If you're okay with hard work, the pay isn't too bad."

"Thank you," Trent replied. "I'll go and check it out when I leave here."

"Leave here right away," the bartender said. "And go get the job, because it won't be available forever. The man whose shoes you have to fill was evidently the one who visited the doctor's clinic this morning."

Trent got to his feet in a hurry. "I'll fetch my things then, and settle my bill," he said.

"Tell old man Kirk Cranston that Billy Wyman said hello," the bartender said.

"Billy Wyman. That your name?" Trent asked.

"It is," Billy answered.

"Well, I'll be on my way, then," Trent said, dropping some money on the counter and turning to leave. "Appreciate the help."

Chapter Three

Trent was branding cattle on his first day at Rock Creek Ranch, when he looked up and saw a young woman surveying him over the fence.

"Are you the new man?" she asked.

Trent tipped his hat and nodded. "Indeed I am, ma'am," he replied gruffly, taken unawares by the raven-haired beauty. Her large, gray eyes watched him calmly as he replied to her question.

"Are you sure you know how to do the job and do it well?" the woman asked, with a slight smile.

Trent tipped his hat again and nodded. "I do indeed, ma'am," he replied, keeping his voice even.

The woman sighed. "Well, I suppose only time will tell if you last out longer than the previous man."

Trent lowered the branding iron and tried not to look too alarmed. He raised his eyebrows questioningly at the woman.

"I don't understand what you mean, ma'am," Trent said.

"The name is Kate, and you are…"

"Luke Grey," Trent said quickly, using the name of a horse he'd one had. "If I may be so bold as to ask, Kate, what exactly did you mean by '*if you last out longer than the last man*'"?

"Oh, my father drives his workers hard, because he drives himself harder," Kate replied, her eyes boldly assessing his body. "But you look strong, so I daresay you'll manage."

"With all due respect, I don't take kindly to being looked over as you would an ox or a horse, ma'am," Trent retorted.

She laughed lightly, and Trent found himself smiling a little, too. "Hmm, you've got fire, apart from muscle. Well now, that could be a good combination, or a potentially dangerous one. Seems to me there's something in the water here that makes our ranch hands so eager and quick to get into fights. You keep a cool head, and you'll be far more productive, Luke Grey," Kate warned him.

Trent shrugged and carried on with his work, aware that Kate was still watching him. She was dressed for riding, with a wide, brown hat and gloves, and her presence was disturbing. Trent noticed her watching him, and it made him aware of his injured arm.

He turned, so that his arm was shielded from Kate's view, and wiped the beads of perspiration off his forehead. As he did so, his eye was drawn to the ranch house, where a shadowy figure appeared to be watching them from one of the windows. Instantly on his guard, Trent kept a subtle eye on the man as he worked. The man stepped back inside and, when he looked up a few minutes later, he was relieved to see Kate had gone as well.

Trent heaved a sigh. He didn't know what he was doing at Rock Creek Ranch. All he wanted was somewhere quiet to hide, and this ranch defeated the purpose. It was large and its owner rich—that could attract trouble. To add to his apprehensions was the looming specter of making a false move and losing his job.

"I'll stay here for a while, make some money, and then be off," Trent said to himself. He continued to lash the fence posts together, repairing the gate that had been broken by a newly captured stallion.

"Good job," a voice said. Trent looked up, meeting his employer's hard green eyes.

"Thank you, Mr. Cranston. It's how I work," Trent said, holding the man's gaze unflinchingly.

"I already like you, Luke Grey," Kirk Cranston said. "You don't seem afraid of me, and you don't seem to be afraid of hard work. My daughter seems to like you, too."

Trent tipped his hat to his boss, who then turned his horse to continue his patrol of the ranch.

Then he stood there a moment, thinking of Kate.

Trent entered the bunkhouse and headed to his bed. This wasn't the kind of accommodation he was used to. The lack of privacy was uncomfortable, but he could handle it. He'd worked on a ranch before.

"Luke Grey!" one of the cowboys hailed him.

"Howdy, Rafe," Trent greeted him without enthusiasm. He wished he could have a room to himself, where he could spend time thinking of what had happened. He still hadn't made sense of the events of the last week, and he needed to make a plan.

He reached under his bed, and then stood up quickly.

"My saddlebag's been opened," Trent growled. "Who's been rifling through my stuff?"

"I did," Rafe replied, giving Trent a challenging look. "We all had questions about you, where you've come from and how you got that wound on your arm that you've been hiding inside your jacket."

"I haven't been hiding anything," Trent snarled, "and if anyone gets into my stuff again, you'll be sorry."

"What're you gonna do? Kill them? You gonna kill me, Luke?" Rafe asked.

"I'm not gonna kill anyone, but I will sure as hell report you to the boss," Trent retorted. "A man's entitled to his privacy. If you want to know something about me, ask me instead of rifling through my things," he added.

"Alright then, where have you come from?" Rafe asked, his arms folded across his chest and his eyes boring into Trent's.

"Wild River County," Trent replied, aware that it was far away enough for Rafe not to know too much about it.

"Oh, really?" Rafe remarked. "And what did you do there?"

"The same thing I'm doing here. Ranching," he answered. "Is that all?"

"For now," Rafe replied. He was clearly not satisfied, but it was dinnertime, and he would rather eat than question Trent any longer.

Trent took his towel off the hook by his bunk bed and went to the outhouse. He washed and changed quickly, and shrugged on his jacket. Then he went to fetch Eagle from the stable on his way to the saloon.

"Where are you headed, Luke Grey?" he heard a familiar voice ask. He turned and saw Kate standing in the doorway.

"The saloon in town, ma'am," Trent replied.

"Can't do without your whiskey, I gather, like all the other cowboys," Kate remarked, sounding vaguely disappointed.

"It's more for the ride and the relaxation," Trent responded, wondering why he felt the need to explain himself.

"Well, you be on your way then," Kate said.

Trent was aware of her eyes on him as he rode away, and he drove his spurs into Eagle's side and galloped faster. He was eager to be away from Rock Creek Ranch for even a few hours.

Sitting at a table at the Lone Mustang some time later, Trent Conway sipped on a glass of whiskey while staring unseeingly into the crowd of people. It still amazed him how small a town White Water was, yet how many people gathered at the saloon all day.

"How is your job going at Rock Creek?" Billy the bartender asked.

"I'm grateful for the work," Trent replied. "And it's going alright, thank you."

"You work hard and do as Kirk Cranston says, Luke Grey, and you'll be just fine," Billy said.

Trent gave the bartender a curious look, a slight shiver going up his spine.

"I'm here to make an honest living," Trent replied. "And I don't intend spoiling my chances of doing just that." He gave Billy a searching look. "What happened to my predecessor? The man who came in injured the day I went to see the doctor?"

Billy guffawed. "What, you worried that he'll be around wanting his job back?" he asked.

Trent shook his head. "No. I'm just wondering what became of him, that's all," he said. "He seemed seriously injured, and the doctor asked him a question that seemed to imply that it wasn't the first time he had come in with injuries of that nature."

"Like I've told you before," Billy warned, "avoid meddling in matters that don't concern you. Just figure he was not a man who did his job well."

"Alright," Trent replied, draining the contents of his glass and getting up to leave.

"Aren't you going to eat something?" Billy asked.

"I'm not hungry," Trent replied, glad of the meal the ranch hands had been served after their day's work.

"Well, I suppose the Cranstons take care of their cowboys," Billy remarked.

Trent acknowledged the observation with a slight nod, and slouched out of the saloon.

Across the street, the doctor's clinic appeared to be open, and Trent decided to pay the medic a visit.

"I just wanted to get my wound checked again," Trent explained, as the doctor raised his eyebrows questioningly.

"I'll take a look," the doctor said, "if you would take your jacket off."

Trent shrugged off his jacket, and the doctor frowned at the wound.

"You shouldn't have exerted your arm so much, so quickly," he said sharply.

"How can you tell I exerted it?" Trent asked.

"Your wound is opening up and bleeding. I need to fix the stitches again," the doctor replied.

"It was my first day on a new job," Trent murmured.

"Yes, that's what they all say," the doctor grumbled.

"What happened to the man who was in your clinic when I came for my last visit?" Trent asked. "Did he say the same thing?"

"I don't keep tabs on my patients," the doctor replied. "And besides, it's not your business at all. My job is to fix them up and send them on their way."

"Of course," Trent answered.

"There are things you will learn about life in these parts," the doctor continued, heaving a deep sigh.

"Billy, the bartender at the saloon, was equally mysterious about this subject," Trent remarked with a tired smile. "And now here you are, saying something similar."

"You do seem like you could use some advice," the doctor said, nodding with a smile.

"So doctor, what advice do you have for me?" Trent asked.

"Take care of your wound, and don't get into any situations that might leave you with more of the same," the doctor said.

"Okay," Trent agreed. He looked at the man through narrowed eyes. He could tell he was holding something back. "And is there anything more I should know?"

"Not really," the doctor said. "Except my name. It's Silas. You can call me Doctor Silas."

Trent got up to leave. "Well, thank you, Doctor Silas," he said, setting some money down on the table. He left the clinic with a prayer that he wouldn't be back with any further wounds.

Chapter Four

"So tell me, Luke Grey, where are you really from?" Kate asked, as she watched Trent break in a particularly difficult mustang.

"Wild River County," Trent replied, his attention on the horse. He was aware that everyone seemed to be asking him questions at odd times, obviously trying to assess whether he was lying. He gave himself a mental pat on the shoulder and heaved a silent sigh of relief at giving Kate the appropriate answer, despite all his energies being focused on the horse.

"And whose ranch did you work on there?" Kate asked, this time catching Trent off guard.

"If you don't mind, ma'am…" he began.

"Kate, if you please," Kate replied firmly.

"If you don't mind, Kate," Trent said, "I'd like to concentrate on the job at hand."

"And I'd like to watch you… and converse at the same time," Kate answered in a teasing voice.

He caught movement from the corner of his eye, and Trent was aware again of someone watching them from one of the windows.

"That's my Ma," Kate said, following Trent's gaze. "She's very protective of me. As she should be, I suppose. I am an only child."

Trent glanced back to the window, and then quickly swung himself up on the horse's back. The horse bucked without warning, and it was all Trent could do to hold on and not fall. Man and beast struggled for control over each other, and Trent prevailed.

"Oh my!" Kate exclaimed, as Trent trotted the horse around the paddock and then came to a halt. "Luke, I know you didn't want me to notice that wound on your arm the other day, but I did notice it. Just as I notice you've kept it concealed under your jacket today. How did it happen, the wound, I mean?"

"I was attacked by a bull," Trent replied quickly.

"I see," Kate murmured. "Show it to me. Maybe I can tell daddy you shouldn't be working, if you are hurt."

Trent shook his head. "I'm sorry, Kate," he said, "but I have to refuse your request. I'm a private sort of guy, and I don't believe in taking my shirt off before a lady."

"I'm your employer, aren't I? Don't my requests count?" Kate asked, crossing her arms.

"If you have a job for me to do, I'll be glad to oblige, ma'am," Trent replied. "But taking off my clothes? No, I'm firm about not doing that."

"Alright then," Kate said, pouting slightly as she moved away.

Trent's eyes flew to the window where Kate's mother stood watching them, and he bit his lip. This was more difficult than he thought it would be.

The frenzied banging on a lid heralded the afternoon meal, and Trent joined the other ranch hands under a tent for a plate of beef, beans and biscuits.

"What's it like having the boss's daughter after you, Luke?" Rafe asked. He followed Trent as he served himself some food and then made his way out of the tent to a trestle table in the sunshine.

"I don't know what you mean," Trent replied, beginning to eat.

"Everybody's talking about how she stands by and watches you at work," Rafe said.

"Oh?" Trent murmured. "Well, I think she was just interested in the mustang I was breaking in."

"Hmm," Rafe responded. "You're a secretive one."

"I've nothing to be secretive about, actually," Trent replied. "And right now, I'd just like to eat in peace if that's alright with you."

"You've been here a month, and nobody really knows anything about you," Rafe remarked. He clearly liked trying to get under Trent's skin.

"I'm sorry," Trent answered wryly. "I'm just not a very interesting person, and I don't have very much to share about myself, really. I'm just a boring old cowboy, that's all."

"So how about that wound, the one you thought nobody noticed?" Rafe asked, giving Trent a challenging look.

"I was attacked by a bull at my last place of work," Trent replied.

"Is that so?" Rafe murmured.

"It *is* so, I'm afraid," Trent answered. "Nothing very interesting or exciting about being attacked by a bull. You work on a ranch. I'm sure you've had your share of injuries from animals."

"If you say so," Rafe drawled, giving Trent a look that said he didn't believe him at all.

Trent chewed on a piece of beef, and suddenly felt a stab of homesickness for Woodson County and his father's ranch. It was a small ranch, but it was theirs, and would have been all his eventually. Working for someone else was all very well, but it meant forfeiting his privacy, and Trent didn't like that at all. He had tried hard not to think of the prospect of never seeing his home again, or his father… all because he had made one tiny mistake.

"Please, Trent," Ellie had begged. "I need you to do this for me… please!"

He had obliged her because she was like the little sister he had never had. He had known Ellie all his life. She was always there at the ranch house, always coming around to ride with him. He had taught her everything she knew about horses because her father, the sheriff, was never around.

"Look, Ellie, Sandy Granger is not a good man. Your dad is right; you need to stop seeing him," Trent had said firmly.

"I love him, Trent. I thought you would understand that. I thought you of all people would be on my side," Ellie had replied.

"You know Ellie, I can't be party to this," Trent had said, stalking off.

"You can't abandon me, Trent," Ellie had said. "Just pretend. Pretend you and I are

together, so that nobody knows it's Sandy I'm with. Just for a while."

"And what happens when everyone gets to know it was all a farce, a cover-up for you being with this man who everybody suspects is a criminal?" Trent had asked.

"Do you care about me, Trent?" Ellie had responded, her face sad.

"I do, Ellie, and that's why I refuse to do as you ask," Trent had said.

And just then, her father had walked in. Without a word, Ellie had thrown herself into Trent's arms and planted her lips firmly on his.

"Oh," Sheriff Anderson had said, and left the room hurriedly.

Word had spread like wildfire that the rancher's son was all but betrothed to the sheriff's daughter.

"It worked! Trent, it worked! And now I can keep meeting Sandy in secret and nobody will suspect a thing. Pa will think I'm with you, and you will keep the story going, won't you Trent?"

Later, while mending the fence on the periphery of Rock Creek Ranch, Trent saw with relief that he was alone. It was just him and his horse. While Eagle cropped the grass, Trent fell to hammering posts in place. He was besieged by memories of happier times, before the murder that had sent him running.

His thoughts were shattered when the cry of a woman in pain rent the air. Trent dropped his tools and jumped on Eagle, much as he had the night that Ellie's screams had come to him from right outside the Conways' ranch. Swiftly banishing the memory, Trent urged Eagle forward and galloped in the direction of the sound.

"Kate!" he cried, spotting her body lying on the ground. "What happened?"

His pulse was racing as he remembered with startling clarity the blood on his hands, shirt… everywhere… when he had picked up Ellie's body and cradled it in his arms.

"You killed her! It was you!" he heard Sandy Granger grind out through clenched teeth.

"I did no such thing. I wasn't even with her," Trent had replied.

"You killed her! You did it!" Sandy roared.

Around him, a crowd gathered, and they all began to chant the words that Sandy was screaming at him.

"Kate!" Trent cried, leaning over Kate's body. He pushed the images of the past from his mind, and concentrated on the now.

"Luke?" Kate murmured. "I got thrown by that mustang you broke in the other day. He threw me and then bolted."

"The horse wasn't ready to ride, Kate," Trent scolded, leaning over to assess her injuries.

"I think I may have hurt my leg really badly," Kate said. "I knew the horse wasn't quite ready, but I wanted to try it out anyway."

"I'd better get you home," Trent said, picking Kate up gently and seating her on his horse.

She fell forward as she tried to shift her weight, gasping out in pain. Carefully, he got up behind her and held her as he took Eagle's reins and rode to the ranch house as fast as he could.

"Where's the mustang now?" Trent asked Kate.

"I don't know, Luke," Kate replied. "I'm sorry, but it ran off. I think it may have jumped that broken part of the fence." She bit off a cry as the horse leaped a small branch and jostled her broken leg.

Trent rode up to the house and jumped off Eagle, then carried her in his arms to the front door, where he knocked loudly.

He heard footsteps running to the door, and then it was thrown open to reveal an older version of Kate. This must be the mother who watched him all the time from a window upstairs, Trent thought to himself.

The woman stood staring at him and Kate, horrified.

"What have you done to my daughter?" the woman demanded.

"Ma, Luke Grey rescued me. I was thrown by a horse," Kate said, wincing in pain as Trent followed his employer's wife into the living room and lay Kate down on a sofa.

"How did you know where to find Kate?" the woman asked Trent, eyeing him suspiciously.

"I was out mending the fence, Mrs. Cranston, when I heard Kate cry out. I found her lying on the ground, injured," Trent replied.

"You may leave now," Kate's mother said. "My husband doesn't approve of us fraternizing with the hired hands."

"Of course," Trent murmured, turning to leave.

"Wait, Luke," Kate said. "I haven't even thanked you properly."

"It's alright, Kate. I was just doing my job," Trent declared.

"You will address my daughter with respect, and refer to her as Miss Cranston," Kate's mother said sharply. "You will by no means get overly familiar with her."

"I'm sorry, ma'am, Mrs. Cranston," Trent apologized hastily.

"I asked Luke to call me by my name, Ma," Kate said irritably. "I wish you and Pa would stop behaving like all the ranch hands were out to do me harm. Luke has just saved my life, and all you can do is be mean to him. It's not right, you know."

"I didn't mean to be ungrateful," Kate's mother said, reluctantly. "I just don't want any trouble."

"I understand, ma'am," Trent said, hurrying towards the door just as Kirk Cranston burst in.

"Kate! What were you thinking, riding off on a mustang that's barely been broken in?" he cried without preamble.

"I know, Pa," Kate replied, shaking her head. "It was a foolish thing to do."

"Thank you, Luke," Kirk Cranston said, turning to Trent and nodding to him. "I'm grateful you were close enough to hear Kate cry out, and that you didn't hesitate in rushing to her rescue."

The man shook his hand, and then Trent tipped his hat and left the house, returning to his task of mending the fence.

"What did you do to impress the boss?" Rafe asked with a curl of his lip, when Trent returned to the bunkhouse at the end of the day.

"I don't know what you mean," Trent said, not pausing as he moved towards his bunk.

"Well, you're to move out of the bunkhouse and get your own cabin," Rafe declared.

Trent's eyebrows shot up in surprise. "This is the first time I'm hearing of this," he remarked. "Perhaps you are mistaken?"

"Yeah, well, I wish I was." Rafe pulled a face and stalked off.

"Luke Grey?" Trent heard a voice call. He turned to see Stan Long, the ranch manager.

"Come with me, please," Stan said.

"Is something wrong?" Trent asked, looking worried.

"On the contrary. You got the boss's attention with your hard work and your resourcefulness. Especially being at the right place at the right time today."

"It was nothing," Trent said.

"Well, you've earned yourself your own cabin, Luke Grey," Stan replied, "and you should be pleased, because that doesn't happen so quickly to anybody."

"I don't mind staying on at the bunkhouse," Trent answered, not wishing to isolate himself further from Rafe and the rest of the ranch hands. He had gotten used to their company—it helped keep him from his darker thoughts.

"The boss has given instructions, and we must follow them, Luke," Stan said firmly. "You can show your appreciation by working harder and doing whatever the boss tells you to. This move bodes well for you, Luke. It means you're marked for greater things, so to speak. You will obviously have the opportunity to make more money as well, if you play your cards right."

Trent gave Luke a searching look, but said nothing. This opportunity was starting to sound like an obligation, too.

"You can get your things now," Stan said. "And I believe you also have your own horse. You can bring it along too. The cabin is at the periphery of the ranch, and has a stable as well. You will be very comfortable there, I'm sure, once you fix it up a bit."

Trent fetched Eagle and joined Stan. The two men mounted their horses and rode to the edge of the ranch where there were a few isolated cabins some distance from each other.

Stan handed Trent a rifle. "Keep this handy. You might need it, Luke," he said. "My cabin is over yonder. If you need anything, just holler."

"Thank you, Stan," Trent replied, unsure of how to take this sudden and unexpected change in his circumstances.

"A word of caution, Luke," Stan said. "Word's been flying around that the boss's daughter has a soft spot for you. That can only mean one thing: trouble. I would maintain my distance if I were you, and I wouldn't encourage her. A lass like that—she's used to having her own way every time, and she might even think of amusing herself with you for a while. It's when she gets bored, or her Ma and Pa begin to hear about the relationship, that things could get ugly. Right now, your job is going well, and you obviously need it, or you wouldn't have traveled some distance to get it. Guard it with your life."

Trent nodded gravely. "Thank you for the advice, Stan. I'll be careful."

"Come on boy," Trent said, leading Eagle into the stall by the cabin after Stan had gone. He swept out the stall and spread out some fresh hay somebody had left for just that purpose, and filled the trough with water. Then he went into the cabin. It was small and compact, with a sofa, a single bed and dresser, and an adjoining room with a stove and a small round table.

Trent fetched a bucket of water and began to clean the rooms. He also washed the plates and pans in the cupboard. When he was done, he went to Eagle and decided to ride into town for some supplies. Much as he liked the food the cook prepared, he was ready to cook for himself. He thought maybe it was time to start thinking, and make a plan. Was it safe to stay here? And did he want to stay?

Chapter Five

Trent lay in his bed and pulled the quilt over him. He heaved a sigh of relief as his eyes closed. He was working hard and his wound had healed. He had successfully managed to keep Kate Cranston at a reasonable distance, and his cabin had begun to feel like home. There wasn't too much else he could ask for.

He was dropping off to sleep when he heard the thunder of horses' hooves. Trent jumped up and went to the window, nudging the curtains aside to look outside. In the silvery moonlight, he could see at least a dozen horsemen pass his cabin and continue on towards Stan's.

It was perfectly normal to see horsemen on a ranch, but Trent felt the hair rise on the back of his neck. He couldn't see what was going on at Stan's cottage, where the horsemen stopped, but there was something altogether strange about the way they turned around and retraced their steps. They passed Trent's cabin and rode close enough for him to see that the horses now carried cargo on their backs. He wasn't sure if they had carried cargo when they were riding to Stan's cottage.

The horsemen were gone as fast as they came, leaving Trent sleepless and restless. Finally, he decided he could report it in the morning, if there were a problem, and lay down in bed and fell asleep.

"Trent! It's Sandy. He needs help. Could you come with me? Please, Trent?"

"Ellie, I told you to be careful of the man. He's obviously up to no good. I can tell that he's only with you because your father is the sheriff, and he hopes you will get your Pa to overlook whatever it is that he's doing illegally."

"You're being rather harsh, Trent, don't you think?"

"I'm being honest, Ellie. I've been hearing a lot about Sandy, and none of it is good. Break it off with him while you can."

"I love him, Trent. Now please, come and help me."

"Ellie, Sandy has been shot. You need to report this to your Pa. Especially since he has been in a gunfight."

"Trent, act like my friend and help me, please. We can do this together."

"I've never taken a bullet out of a man's body before, Ellie. What if he bleeds to death?"

"He won't. Here, take his knife and sterilize it in the fire. We can do this, Trent."

"I'm doing this for you, Ellie, and not for Sandy. I don't approve of this man, and this is the last time I'm going to do anything for him."

Trent woke in a cold sweat and sat up in bed, gasping for breath. He could feel the noose around his neck again, and his mind went back to the dream he had just pulled himself from.

"Ellie! Oh, Ellie," he gasped. "Why didn't you listen to me? Now look what's happened."

"Trent," he could hear Ellie say. "What are you saying? I don't think you're being fair to Sandy. I'm sure he's not involved in anything illegal, like you're implying he is."

"I'm going to find out, Ellie, and when I do, you'll know that you should've listened to me."

"Sandy says you just want to poison my mind against him, because you want me for yourself, Trent."

"Ellie, stop being absurd. You've always been like my little sister, you know that. I can't stand to see you setting yourself up for a fall. Ellie, listen to me, please."

"Luke! Luke Grey!" Kate called out as he left his cabin.

Trent turned to face her. He had not gotten back to sleep after his restless dreams, and so he had decided to start checking on the horses early. He had a particular horse he was looking forward to riding.

"You're up early, ma'am," Trent observed.

"Kate," Kate corrected him, pouting prettily. "I heard you're breaking in the white mustang today, and I want to watch you. I want the horse for myself. Pa said I could have him," she continued.

"It's a spirited horse, Kate, and it hasn't been so long since you took a toss," Trent warned her.

"I'm a brave girl, Luke," Kate said, flashing a lovely smile. "And I'm sure the horse will be perfectly well behaved after you've worked with him. I shall also promise to be patient this time around and not attempt to ride the horse until you tell me it's safe to do so."

They were almost at the corral when Trent saw Kirk Cranston burst out of the house and stride purposefully towards him and Kate. He took an instinctive step away from her, putting a little distance between himself and the boss's daughter.

"Luke," Kirk Cranston said, "just the man I was looking for."

"Oh, Pa," Kate pouted, "Luke was going to break in the white mustang, and now you're going to give him something else to do, aren't you?"

"As a matter of fact, I am," Kirk said. "Luke can work on the mustang later, and you shall have it as I promised you would, Kate. But right now there are more important matters to attend to." He turned to Trent.

"Luke, I need you to pack your saddlebag and get your horse—or take one of mine. You need to accompany a wagon of our farm produce," Kirk Cranston said.

"To the market?" Trent asked.

"To a private buyer," Kirk Cranston replied, with a sharp look.

Trent felt the hairs rise on the back of his neck again. But he had no good reason to say no, and so he nodded.

"Alright, then," Kirk Cranston said. "Let's get you on your way."

Trent turned to follow his boss, leaving Kate looking disappointed. He wanted to ask what the produce was, but his instincts warned him to ask no questions. His position was vulnerable, and he just had to do what his boss asked of him.

"Oh, there you are, Luke," Stan said. Trent had followed Kirk's directions and found his way to a barn where Stan and some of the other ranch hands were loading a wagon. Trent tried not to look too curious, but he could see that whatever was being loaded into the wagon was not farm produce. Whatever it was, it was packed in lumpy bags. It was light, whatever it was, because the fully bags were still easily lifted by one man.

"You'll be one of the four of us going with the wagon," Stan said, not looking Trent directly in the eye.

Trent nodded without a word.

"Good that you've got your own horse," Stan observed. "It's good to ride a horse that you're comfortable with and that can anticipate your every move. I hope you've got the rifle I gave you."

"I have my pistols," Trent said. "I can carry the rifle as well, if you suggest I do."

"I think you should," Stan said, handing Trent a cartridge belt. "And don't forget, no talking. I will hand over the goods, and we will leave soon after."

Trent took the belt and exchanged it with the one he was wearing. Stan gave him a nod of approval, as if silently applauding him for not asking any questions.

As they rode away, Trent saw a figure by a window. Kirk Cranston's wife was watching him.

"You take the left with Craig, and I'll take the right of the wagon with Mark," Stan instructed Trent. "And pull your bandanas up, boys."

Trent nodded and fell to the left of the wagon with the ranch hand he recognized as Craig, tying his bandana over his face as he did so.

Craig threw Trent an uncertain look. His face was ashen above his bandana.

"You okay, Craig?" Trent asked in a low voice so that Stan couldn't hear.

"It's my first time. What about you?" Craig replied.

Trent said nothing. He was wondering what the mission was, and how dangerous it would be.

"My first time too," Trent declared.

"Oh, really?" Craig remarked. "Well, let's just one we're both good shots."

Trent rode in silence after that, wondering what the wagon really contained, and what he was about to get himself into.

"We're almost at the handover point," Stan said, riding up alongside Trent and Craig. Trent could see Craig blink rapidly, and his own heartbeat accelerated.

Stan rode back to his side as the trail narrowed. The wagon bumped along the rocky stretch, the horse's hooves slipping on the rubble.

Trent glanced up at the banks on either side, alerted by a movement in the undergrowth just above. Before he could sound a warning, however, he saw the bullets come at them. Trent grabbed his pistols and fired back, rising up in the stirrups to take better aim at their attackers.

"What the…?" Stan hollered, taking aim with his rifle. The firing momentarily ceased, and then began again.

"Halt!" someone above them roared. Trent saw, to his horror, men coming at them in a flurry of gravel from the banks on either side. He let fly with both pistols. He saw Craig fall trembling to the ground, and covered him and the wagon simultaneously.

He jumped in front of the wagon and was fighting off the onslaught from the front when he saw a familiar pair of eyes peering into his. An all-too-familiar face appeared in front of him, and Trent almost dropped his pistols, his fingers freezing on the triggers momentarily.

It was Sandy Granger.

"Get back!" he heard Stan cry. "Now cover the wagon while I return to the ranch and report to the boss."

Stan was shouting into his ear, and Trent was nodding rapidly, not letting up with his pistols. His hands were trembling at the sight of Sandy Granger so close to him. Though most of Trent's face was covered with his bandana, Trent feared he may have been recognized. But now he had to focus on the battle at hand.

As Stan rode off with the wagon, Trent and Mark kept up the fire until they were sure Stan had put a considerable distance between them. When their assailants gave up, Trent turned his attention to Craig.

"Craig!" Trent shouted. "Craig! Get up!"

Craig was hit and bleeding, and Trent and Mark lifted him up onto his horse and rode back to the ranch with him.

Kirk Cranston greeted them with the merest nod, casting a withering look at Craig's inert, bleeding body.

"We were attacked," Trent said by way of explanation.

"It's to be expected," Kirk replied.

"Stan managed to get the wagon away safely, and asked us to return to the ranch," Trent added.

"Alright, then," Kirk said. "You can return to your work and say nothing more of what happened."

Later that day when Trent returned to his cabin, he saw Stan's horse had returned. He caught a brief glimpse of Stan on his porch.

Trent went into his cabin and bolted the door behind him, then sank into the sofa and leaned back as he exhaled. He had seen Sandy Granger. Sandy could have possibly recognized him. How long would he be safe at Rock Creek Ranch? His thoughts flew to Craig, then, and Kirk's indifference to his employee's injuries. Trent and Mark had bathed his wound and bound it, and left Craig resting in the bunkhouse.

A knock on the door brought Trent to his feet. His hand slipped automatically onto his holster.

"Who is it?" Trent asked sharply.

"Luke, it's me, Craig," a voice weakly replied.

"Craig?" Trent queried, opening the door. "What's going on? You should be resting."

"I was," Craig replied, wincing in pain, "but Stan came by and said that the boss had relieved me of my duties at the ranch, so I'm leaving."

"But you're injured," Trent remarked, "and it's not your fault that you fell today."

"I'm not strong or brave, Luke," Craig replied. "I was scared out of my wits when those bullets came at us." He raked his fingers through his hair. "I don't know where to go, but I have to leave now."

Trent gave Craig a sympathetic look. "I wish I could help," he said.

"You did, Luke," Craig replied. "You and Mark brought me back and bandaged up my wound. I just came by to thank you."

After Craig had left, Trent returned to his sofa and sank into it with his head in his hands. What kind of man fires a man when he's hurt?

Trent got up and prepared his evening meal: beans and biscuits and a mug of coffee. He wolfed it down, then he got onto Eagle and rode into town.

The Lone Mustang Saloon was full. Trent got himself a glass of whiskey and then escaped to a shadowy corner. He sat down to drink it while mulling over the events of the day.

"So, old Cranston seems pleased with you," Billy Wyman said, coming up to Trent's table.

"Is he?" Trent said.

"Yes, word goes around, you know," Billy replied. "Apparently you're just the man he's been looking for. You know where the money comes from."

"Maybe I do," Trent nodded to Billy and took a large sip of whiskey from his glass.

"You hear about those men got shot the other day?" Billy remarked.

"Nope. I just got in from the ranch. Not a lot of news out there," Trent replied. He was aware that Billy was trying to get information which he wasn't going to provide.

"So, have you been given any interesting tasks lately?" Billy asked.

Trent squinted at the contents of his glass. "Depends on what you mean by interesting, Billy," he said. "If you mean breaking in horses and mending fences, then yep, I suppose I've been up to plenty of that."

"I see," Billy said, giving Trent a narrow look. "Someone from the Cranston's ranch came in earlier, a man called Craig Thomson. He was injured and went across the street to the doctor."

"Oh," Trent murmured. "Perhaps he was thrown from his horse… or attacked by an angry bull?"

"Looked more like a bullet wound to me," Billy said, his eyes still searching Trent's face for answers. "But you wouldn't know anything about that, would you? Even with you working out at that ranch?"

Trent shook his head. "Can't say I do," he replied. "I'm sorry for Craig, though. I know what it feels like to be running from an irate bull, only to be backed up against a fence or a wall and have to fight for your life."

Billy shook his head slowly from side to side with a slight smile on his face.

"You learn fast, Luke Grey," he said. "I can see why Kirk Cranston is so pleased with you." Billy Wyman laughed and returned to the bar counter, and Trent drained the contents of his glass and left.

Walking out into the street, Trent saw a group of men conversing. Not feeling safe in crowds now, he dropped his head and walked with his shoulders stooped so that it wasn't easy to look into his face. He untied Eagle quickly from the hitching rail and climbed onto the horse, observing with some apprehension that the men were looking at him.

"You seem in a hurry, cowboy," one of the men said, striding purposefully up to him.

"I don't see how that's anybody's business but mine," Trent shot back

"Ah," the man said, "I was told you were not the talker. I have come to you with an offer."

Trent looked the man squarely in the eye. "What kind of offer? And who told you anything?" he asked.

"Your employer told me to watch you, and determine if you were the right man for the job."

"So," Trent said, watching the man's face, "you've been shadowing me? So why do you claim this now, and admit it?" He was worried—there were a lot of people looking for him. But he decided to play this on the man's terms, for now.

"I felt it was the right time," the man answered. "I was asked to follow you and then, if I felt like I could trust you, to have you follow us. We have a delivery for you to make."

"Well," Trent replied, "I'm not willing to follow anyone until I know what I'm following into. I would need some more information."

"Is this enough information?" the man asked, whipping out his gun.

Trent looked at the man calmly from under his hat. "Now look here, are you trying to threaten me?"

"Just using some good old fashioned motivation, is what I'm doing," the man drawled, shooting into the air.

"Well, if it's a fight you want," Trent said, his hands moving to his guns, "then a fight you shall have."

The man pointed his gun at him. "The last shot was in the air. This one will show you who has the upper hand," he declared.

"Oh?" Trent said. He leaped off Eagle with a well-aimed kick, dropping his adversary to the ground. He had the man's hands pinned down and a pistol to his head in a trice, and was wresting his gun from him when he realized that the other men had surrounded him.

Trent gauged his opponents with a practiced eye, then jumped to his feet and shot in their general direction as he ran into the narrow alley. He heard a yelp of pain, and then the sound of footsteps. Trent hid quickly, in a dark doorway, and watched as the men ran right past him.

He returned to the street, where he realized that Eagle had fled the scene. Trent inserted his forefingers into his mouth and whistled, and Eagle galloped out of a dark corner. Trent mounted him quickly and was about to ride off, when a figure stepped into his path.

It was Stan Long.

"Luke, who were those men?" Stan asked.

"I don't know," Trent replied. "They accosted me, and one of them tried to get me to do something for him. He also told me he had been asked to shadow me."

"By?" Stan asked.

"By the boss," Trent replied. "Somehow I didn't believe anything he said, and I refused to do as he asked, so he opened fire. Well, he fired over my head."

"What did he ask you to do?" Stan asked.

"Follow him," Trent answered. "But I don't know where it was that he was asking me to go.

And then make a delivery. I didn't know that man, and I didn't think the orders came from the boss."

"They didn't," Stan said. "They came from me."

"What!" Trent exclaimed, aghast.

"I always test the new men. Need to be sure about them, you know," Stan said. "I was also glad to see that you did not at first shoot to kill. My men are told to only threaten, and not return fire if possible."

"Oh… I see," Trent replied, not sure whether to be relieved or further distressed. He was glad he had not killed anyone, this time.

"You passed," Stan declared. "You proved you are reliable and good at a fight." He grinned. "The boss likes to be sure. It was part of the plan. You see, we needed to pick our men for the cattle drive. So now, go back to your cabin and get some rest. Because tomorrow we head out early."

"A cattle drive?" Trent said. "This is the first I've heard of this. We barely have fifteen head of cattle at the ranch. Why would we travel with so few?"

"Well," Stan said, giving Trent one of his enigmatic looks. "This is a bit different. You see, we have to go and bring the cattle here. And it's a journey that's quite challenging. Which is why we needed to assess our team of men. Now Luke, no more questions. Go and rest."

Trent blanched as a thought struck him. He had a feeling that robbery the other day had not been quite what he had though. Stan had not mentioned it, and there was clearly something fishy going on with this reverse cattle drive.

He just couldn't shake the feeling that Sandy Granger was in on something with Kirk Cranston and Stan Long.

Trotting back to his cabin, Trent was surprised to see Kate waving to him. He dismounted as he reached her.

"Luke," Kate said, "I missed you today."

Trent looked at her smiling face, and realized he believed she genuinely meant what she was saying.

"I'm sorry, your father needed me to do something for him," Trent replied.

"I know. And I missed watching you break in the mustang," Kate said. "But I can watch you tomorrow, can't I?"

"Actually Kate," Trent said, "I am to leave with some of the men quite early in the morning to go on a cattle drive."

"Oh!" Kate exclaimed, her disappointment apparent. "I didn't know about it."

"I only just got to know a little while ago," Trent said. His eyes went to a window in the house. "Your Ma is anxiously watching us, as usual, by the way."

Kate shrugged. "I don't really care if she does," she said. "I'm a grown woman and can do as I like."

"Can you really?" Trent asked.

Kate nodded with a smile. "Well, usually. I do have to follow the rules of the house, and I would not want you to get in trouble. But we are just talking, and that is not too scandalous, is it?"

"I believe you are correct, Kate," Trent said. "I'm sorry to have missed seeing you today, as well. After I get some food and some rest, I promise I will be back and will break in the white horse for you."

"Good. And please, don't be afraid of my parents," Kate said. "I won't let them get in the way." Kate blushed suddenly, as if her words had surprised her. "I'd better go now," she said.

Trent tipped his hat to her and mounted Eagle. That night he slept fitfully, the weight of the cattle drive already upon him.

Chapter Six

They set off without much fanfare early the next morning. The men were struggling to appear alert and many were still rubbing the sleep from their eyes.

"While you were asleep, we were getting prepared," Stan explained, as Trent looked around him at the group of over twenty horses. He was happy to see a chuckwagon also loaded and ready to go.

Stan scrutinized Trent's attire. "Good, you're dressed appropriately. Chaps and all," he said.

Trent nodded.

"Pull your bandana up and keep it up through the ride," Stan instructed.

Trent pulled up his bandana. He jumped onto Eagle and joined the other men.

"What is our destination?" one of the men asked Stan.

"You'll know when we reach it," Stan replied. "Have you all got your pistols loaded and your extra ammo packed?"

The men nodded. Some of them were looking apprehensive, and Trent wondered how the expedition would pan out.

They stopped only twice for sustenance from the chuck wagon and to relieve themselves along the trail. The journey was otherwise relentless, and Trent began to wish he had left Eagle at the ranch.

"Right, now we're going to stop for a rest," Stan said.

"Don't we get to sleep?" Trent heard a voice ask hopefully.

"You may nap for an hour or two, and then we begin the operation," Stan replied.

"The operation?" someone else asked.

"Yes. Now, no more questions. We eat, rest, relieve ourselves, and get ready. We will be picking up roughly five hundred head of cattle, and we are twenty of us. Each of us is in charge of a herd of twenty-five cattle. Lose any, and you're in trouble. Get every one of your cattle safely to Rock Creek Ranch, and you earn yourself a bonus. Remember, this is a risky mission. There will be a fight involved. We need to get the cattle from a guarded enclosure. Ask no questions and just do as you're told."

Trent was sure now he had gotten himself in deep. It became increasingly obvious to him that this mission was not an honest one. They were not buying cattle and herding them back. They were stealing them. And if he got caught doing that, the law would probably find out about his murder charge, too.

He looked around the landscape and contemplated a quick escape.

"And don't be getting any funny ideas about running away, just because the mission doesn't seem all that exciting to you," Stan said, as if reading Trent's thoughts. "Remember, there's a reward at the end of it."

Trent sat down with a plate of beans and biscuits and a tin mug of coffee and stared out at the horizon, wondering if Sandy Granger was going to put in an appearance somewhere along the trail. The thought made him uncomfortable, and he finished eating quickly and pulled his bandana up over his face.

It was past midnight when the twenty men mounted their horses, left the rest of the horses and the chuck wagon along the trail, and made their way furtively towards the fence of what appeared to be a very large ranch.

"We have men on the inside who will let us in," Stan said. "We work fast, rounding up twenty-five cattle each and getting them back here. We then pick up the rest of the horses and the chuck wagon, and we travel back as fast as we can."

Under his bandana, Trent bit his lip. The mission sounded simple enough, but he was uneasy.

"Right men, now keep your eyes on the cattle, you hear?" Stan instructed.

There were nods and grunts, but the men were otherwise silent – each probably wrestling with his own misgivings about being a part of such an operation.

As they approached the fence, Trent saw a group of men riding towards them. One of them dismounted and took apart a section of the fence to let them through. No words were exchanged, and everyone was silent, the only sound being that of the horses' hooves on the soft grass beneath them.

They followed the men who had let them in, and found their way to a paddock filled with cattle.

One of the inside men opened the paddock gate, and the cattle swarmed out. The cowboys counted out twenty-five each and herded them out towards the gap in the fence.

Trent watched the action, and then gave a sharp intake of breath. He saw, in the moonlight, bodies of dogs lying inert by the paddock fence. He realized that the inside men had shot them to get rid of them. Trent felt like his lungs had no air left in them, such was his anger at the scene. Taking a rich man's cows did not bother him, but there was rarely a good reason to shoot a dog.

The cowboys filed out, each with their herd of cattle, and started up the slope towards the place where they had left the rest of their horses and the chuck wagon. That was when the first shots rang out. Someone had sounded an alarm inside the ranch. Trent saw lamps bobbing in the semi-darkness, and heard the drumming of horses' hooves. He felt the bile rise in his gut again. They were going to have to fight the owners for their cattle, and it wasn't the fight that made him sick, but the fact that he was now a cattle thief.

"This way!" Trent heard a voice say, and froze. It was Sandy Granger's voice.

"They're close," Stan said, turning around. Trent followed his gaze and drew his pistols.

Stan pointed. "Luke, you and Mark come with me. We will keep those men off while the rest of you go!"

Trent herded his cattle further up the slope and rejoined Stan, pistols drawn and poised to shoot.

The first bullet took him by surprise, and Trent ducked just in time. He opened fire with both pistols simultaneously and saw his targets buckle and fall, but others came at them. Trent stood his ground, and then saw that the men were going after the cattle, trying desperately to retrieve them and drive them back to the paddock. There was momentary mayhem as Stan barked out orders and they fought the cattle owners, pushing them back as they moved the cattle further.

"Maim or kill," Stan cried. "We have to get going!"

Trent felt a bullet graze his cheek and a trickle of blood beneath the bandana. Maim or kill, the words echoed. He would do what he had to do. A man came at him, and Trent shot him at point-blank range, evading a bullet as he did so. He shot another in the side. He heard cries of anguish and saw men crumple up into heaps of bloody flesh, and still he fought on.

"You will pay for this!" Trent heard one of the men roar. The rightful owners of the cattle he was stealing.

"We'll get you!" someone else cried.

"Now, time to run!" Stan said. "Go!"

Trent turned Eagle about and followed Stan, when a shot rang out and a bullet grazed his shoulder. He cried out and clutched his arm, but kept going.

"Mark is down!" Stan cried, pointing at a body on the trail.

Trent pulled Eagle up and jumped off, running towards the body he had seen falling from the horse.

"Leave him!" Stan roared. But Trent hooked his hands under Mark's arms, biting back his own pain, and heaved his body up the slope.

Swearing and cursing, Stan jumped off his horse and helped Trent lift Mark onto Eagle. Then Trent got on behind him and galloped after the others.

Some miles up the trail, they stopped. Trent pulled Mark off Eagle and examined his wound, using alcohol and a spare bandana to treat and bind it. He the blood and rendered Mark fit to travel the rest of the way.

"Luckily it's not too far back to the ranch," Trent remarked.

Stan cleared his throat. "Well, Luke, actually we're not taking the cattle back to Rock Creek. We have to take them to the market, and that's a whole three days' journey."

"Oh," Trent said.

"And that's why I didn't want you to rescue Mark. But you were being a hero, and I let you," Stan said dryly.

"Surely we couldn't leave him there?" Trent asked incredulously.

"We do what we have to, Luke. Each man for himself and every man for the cattle," Stan declared. "Now, you're going to be hampered by having to take care of Mark along the trail."

"I'll get better, Stan," Mark spoke up. "I'll be fine once my dang leg stops hurting so much."

"If we pass through a town, maybe we can find a doctor," Trent said hopefully.

"We're not passing through any towns, Luke," Stan said. "This is wilderness all the way to the place where we hand over the cattle and get paid. So as for Mark, he's now your problem."

"Where are the men who helped us get inside the ranch?" Trent asked Stan a while later.

"They've gone back, of course," Stan replied, and Trent heaved a sigh of relief.

"Look, I'm not as hard-hearted as you probably think I am," Stan said. "I have known Mark longer than you have, but we need to be practical at times like these."

"Yes, of course," Trent said.

Stan looked at Mark and sighed. "I'll talk to the cook and see if he can find some room in the chuck wagon. Then Mark could ride in there," he said.

"Thank, Stan," Mark said. "I'm sure I'll be fine."

It was close to dawn and the cowboys were tired. Keeping the cattle together was hard, even when it was just twenty-five head apiece. Trent could see spirits sag around him, but Stan was relentless in driving them forward.

"Come daylight and the dangers increase. Those men from the ranch could pursue us. Even though we've taken an unplanned route, we're still vulnerable," he said.

"We need to eat," one of the men said. "Or at least get a drink of water. Our horses are flagging."

"Change them, then. That's what all these extra horses are for," Stan barked.

Trent stroked Eagle's mane. He wasn't going to change horses. Eagle was as close as he could get to normalcy in the face of this madness, and he wasn't going to give him up, even for a while. He was glad when Mark was laid in the chuck wagon and some of the provisions were tied onto the spare horses. It had been difficult for Eagle to carry both Trent and Mark, but the horse had borne up remarkably well.

"There's a river ahead," someone remarked. "Could we stop, Stan?"

"No. We cross it, and believe me, it's going to be tough," Stan replied.

Trent looked at the tumbling surface of the water and shivered in anticipation. The water was going to be uncomfortably cold, and they would have to bear it.

"We should try and find a way around the river," Trent ventured to suggest. "Or a shallower place."

"We don't have time for that, Luke," Stan shot back. "We need to press on and get to our waiting customers. These cattle are only going to get harder to keep together."

He turned to face the group of men behind them. "Dwight!" Stan called out. "Go in and cross first. We'll follow!"

Trent galloped to the bank of the river and watched the cowboy called Dwight go in on his horse. The horse waded in awkwardly, sliding on the sloping floor of the riverbed, and then began to falter.

"Take off your holster and guns and tie them around your neck!" Stan cried. "Keep your guns dry."

Dwight and the rest of the men followed Stan's instructions. Dwight slid off his horse and walked into the water, leading his horse and driving his twenty-five cattle. He was waist-deep by the middle of the river, and Stan gave the orders for the others to follow.

Trent was perhaps the first to see the men hiding along the rocky stretch on the other side of the river. He turned to Stan, just as the other man yelled a warning.

"They have come for the cattle!" Stan roared, plunging into the water and yelling to Trent to hurry towards them.

Trent took the offensive immediately. Whipping out his rifle, began to fire at the men. He tried to wound them, but he knew it was down to his life or theirs.

As Dwight drove his cattle in front of him, the other men began to snatch them as they crossed to the other side. Dwight fired at the men, but was unsteady in the water and missed his targets. The men were laughing gleefully, receiving the cattle at the other end and herding them away, while Dwight was struggling.

"You lose your cattle, you lose your head, Dwight!" Stan shouted.

Trent made a hasty move, which paid off in the end. He left his cattle in the middle of the lake and plunged in to help Dwight. Eagle splashed through the water as Trent let fly with his rifle. He reached the other side of the lake and fired at the cattle thieves from close range. The cattle thieves scattered.

Emboldened and spurred on by Trent, the other cowboys jumped into the fray, rescued Dwight's cattle and chased the thieves away.

"That wasn't very wise of you, Luke," Stan chastised Trent. "You took an enormous risk and almost lost us our men. I thought I emphasized *each man for himself.*"

"Yes, but you also said, *and every man for the cattle,*" Trent reminded Stan. "I just did what I felt I needed to do."

"You have a problem, Luke. You think you're some kind of hero, don't you?"

"No," Trent said. "I just feel it's the least one can do for a fellow cowboy."

"Well, nobody's going to come to your aid when you're in trouble, Luke. You know that, don't you?"

Trent shrugged. "I hope someone might," he answered.

"One word of warning, Luke Grey," Stan said, "don't be too soft. This is a hard life, on a hard road. You'll need to learn to be tough if you want to stay alive."

Chapter Seven

"We have to push on," Stan told the men, who looked mutinous. They had forded the river and were cold and wet.

"We need to get out of our wet clothes and dry off. Some of us haven't brought a change," Dwight said.

Stan ignored him and addressed the men. "If you have a change of clothes, you get two minutes to get out of your wet things… otherwise, toughen up and behave like men."

Trent bit back a retort and left his wet clothes on. The breeze would dry out his trousers, and he was tall, so the water hadn't reached further than his thighs. He was anxious to get going, and even more eager to return to Rock Creek Ranch, hand in his notice and leave.

"Let's move!" Stan ordered, and the men climbed reluctantly onto their horses and set off. Morale dropped further when the cook announced that a bundle of flour that had been strapped onto one of the horses, in order to accommodate Mark in the wagon, had been lost in the river.

"No flour, no biscuits," somebody grumbled.

Trent thought longingly of his own home and felt a pang of regret.

"Alright men, we're stopping for our evening meal and an hour or two of rest. Then we keep going," Stan said.

"That's inhuman!" one of the men declared.

"It's called hard work," Stan retorted. "Something that you obviously know very little about."

Trent finished his plate of beans quickly and washed it down with a mug of coffee. Then he lay down to get some rest, choosing a spot a little way away from the others and deciding to make the most of the two hours they were allowed to sleep. He was halfway into his two hours when he felt a finger prod him in the ribs. A voice called his name in a conspiratorial whisper.

"Trent," he heard a familiar voice say. He sprang up, drawing his pistols and aiming them at the man who was standing before him.

"The name's Luke Grey," Trent said, fighting to keep his voice steady.

"Look, I know who you are, and you know who I am. So it is vital that we both keep each other's secret. There's something else you need to know," his visitor replied.

Trent knew who he was immediately. "Sandy Granger, I recognized you the moment I heard your voice. You are nothing but a murderer who framed me, and I'm on the run under an alias. But you know damn well that I'm innocent of Ellie's blood," Trent said, his voice trembling with emotion.

"Keep your voice down, Trent. We don't want our covers blown," Sandy whispered.

"Who's to prevent me from putting a bullet through you right here, right now?" Trent shot back.

"You won't be so stupid as to do that, will you, Trent? At least not before hearing my side of the story," Sandy replied.

Trent waved his pistols in Sandy's direction. "I don't want to listen to one word that comes out of your lying lips, you murderer," he said.

"Now, now, Trent. I understand that you might feel antagonistic towards me. I did, after all, accuse you of a murder you didn't commit. But I had my reasons," Sandy continued, ignoring Trent's refusal to listen to him. "You might not believe it, but I did it in order to draw out the real murderer."

"Which is you," Trent snarled.

"Look, what you're involved in is a pretty nasty operation," Sandy declared.

"And I don't need you to tell me so," Trent retorted. "You're part of it. I saw you open the gates to the ranch."

"It's all part of my cover," Sandy said. "You have to believe me, Trent."

"You killed Ellie," Trent shot back, his voice hard. "And I will never forgive you for it. You made me give up my life and take on a new identity. I'm a fugitive, thanks to you!"

"The plan misfired because you ran, Trent. You were supposed to get caught and put in jail, locked up for your own safety. You see, there are people after you because they think that you know what Ellie knew. Little do they know, that it is I who hold the secret."

"Nothing of what you're saying makes sense, Sandy Granger, so why don't you get out of here before I start shooting," Trent said.

"Don't be a fool, Trent. Listen to me," Sandy said, stepping forward.

"Take one more step towards me, and you're dead, Sandy," Trent snarled.

"You'll wake the men. You'll wake Stan," Sandy said. "Just listen to me. Take good care that you don't blow either my cover or yours. Believe it or not, I'm your ally, not your enemy. I loved Ellie deeply, and she loved me. Yes, I know how suspicious of me you were, because Ellie told me so. But you saved my life, Trent Conway, and I owe you one."

"You don't owe me anything, murderer," Trent snarled. "You are no ally. You ruined my life," Trent said. "And I saved your life for Ellie. I did it for her, not for you."

"Whoever you did it for, Trent," Sandy said, "I am grateful. Deeply grateful. You will realize, by and by, that I am not your enemy. You will realize that what I did, I had to do."

"The fact is, Sandy," Trent said, "Ellie's gone and you're here. It should be the other way around."

"Time to get packing, boys!" Stan called from the other side of the camp, interrupting their whispered conversation.

"I have to leave," Sandy said. "I can't be discovered. I've been following you all. But only you know this now."

"I'll get you, Sandy. I'll make you pay," Trent said, as Sandy turned to leave.

Sandy paused. "We'll talk later, Trent," he said. "In the meantime, be careful."

"No, Sandy," Trent retorted. "You be careful. Watch out. Because when I get the opportunity and have you alone, I will take you out."

As the cowboys set off again, each minding his twenty-five head of cattle, Trent seethed with righteous anger. This was wrong, the way Sandy shrugged off any responsibility for Ellie's death. And what did he mean, he was undercover, too? It must be some sort of trick, and he would get to the bottom of it, Trent resolved. Somehow, Sandy had traveled all the way from Woodson County and ended up right where he was. Trent shivered. Had Sandy been following him all along? Right from Woodson County?

He had heard the gunshots before anyone else. Except that he didn't know who had fallen before the bullets. But he soon learned. Poor Ellie had become the target for an unscrupulous man who would do anything to escape the Law.

"What's going on?" Trent had cried, racing past his father and running out into the night.

"I heard shots, Trent," his father had replied. "I'll check on the horses, you check the cattle."

"What are you up to, Sandy?" Trent said, under his breath. He had calmed down enough to wonder why Sandy hadn't arrested him and taken him to be hanged as he had threatened to do when he set the marshals and the sheriff on him. Could it be that Sandy was really on his side? But no, how could he be?

"Something wrong, Luke?" Stan asked, riding alongside him.

"Luke! Luke?"

Stan was shouting as they rode along, and the other cowboys turned to stare questioningly at him.

"I'm fine, just woolgathering," Trent responded. He realized he hadn't reacted to Stan's use of his name. That was because just earlier, Sandy had addressed him by his real name. For a moment, he had almost forgotten that he was meant to be someone called Luke Grey.

Stan looked at him. "Let's get ready to water the horses and cattle soon, before pressing on."

"We can't go further," one of the men interrupted. "It's pitch dark and our lanterns are inadequate. Besides, anyone could see us before we see them, and that's a risk."

"We push on regardless," Stan declared firmly. "No stopping for anything or anyone. If we're attacked, we fight, and we take care that none of the cattle are lost."

Trent looked out at the dark landscape, his eyes boring into the shadows. Riding with their lanterns to light the path ahead of them was definitely a risk, and Trent felt the hairs rise on the back of his neck as they usually did when he sensed danger. He drew a pistol and held it poised, and then he heard it again lower.

A quiet cry, cutting through the sound of horses' hooves and the slight clatter of the chuck wagon.

"It sounds like a woman," Trent said. Stan was right by his side, and reacted immediately.

"It may be, but it could also be a trick. None of your heroics, Luke," he warned.

Trent glowered at Stan in the darkness and said nothing.

The cry reached their ears again, and Trent felt the urge to race towards it.

"It could be someone injured or close to death," he said to Stan. "Would it be right to leave them there alone?"

"We don't borrow any more trouble than we already have on the trail, Luke, you hear?" Stan barked.

Trent began to answer, when a host of shadowy figures came at them. He drew his second pistol and began to fire with both guns, using what brush there was for cover. He was aware of Stan shouting out instructions for half of the company to veer away to the left and herd the cattle to safety, while the rest of them fight off the assailants.

Trent dodged to avoid a bullet, when he realized that the men who were attacking them didn't appear to be interested in the cattle. They seemed to be looking for someone, peering into each man's face. Trent was glad he had pulled his bandana up and that only his eyes were visible.

He felt a surge of indignation. It was obvious Sandy Granger was behind this attack. Why else would they be looking for anybody? He was going to try and kill Trent and make it seem like an attack by brigands.

With a loud cry, Trent tore past the horsemen, looking for Sandy. A bullet grazed his leg, and Trent shot a man in the head. He watched him fall from his horse, and cause another horse to stumble. He saw that while there may be a lot of them, the men were not very good shots. It was quite easy to take them down.

Trent saw a surprising flash of color on a passing horse, and he realized who had been behind the cry in the night. It was a young woman, being held captive by one of the men.

"Don't be a fool, Luke!" Stan yelled at him as Trent went to the woman's rescue.

"Let the woman go, you varmints!" Trent roared. "Cowards! That you would harm a woman so!"

"Stop it, Luke!" Stan cautioned him as he exchanged fire with one of the attackers.

"I'm not going to shirk my duty as a man of honor, Stan," Trent retorted. He jumped off Eagle and onto the ground, landing on his feet with practiced ease. He pulled his rifle off Eagle and took his aggressors on with it, releasing a volley of shots that threw them into confusion.

"Help!" the woman cried. Trent ran towards the horse on which she was being held, sinking a well-aimed bullet into her captor's temple.

"Take the horse and run!" Trent instructed the woman, watching her gallop away.

One of their attackers rode up behind Trent and tore the bandana off his face. Trent bit down on the man's hand and slammed the butt of his rifle into the man's eye. The man howled in pain and Trent unhorsed him with a shot in his arm, and fled. He had lost his lantern in the scuffle and now had to follow the tiny flames bobbing up and down ahead of him. He hoped it was Stan and the cowboys he was following and not the remnants of the gang of attackers.

All of a sudden, he was caught off guard by a horse that came careening at him. Trent drove his spurs into Eagle's side and tried to veer away, but the horse blocked his path. He stared as the woman he had rescued moments ago addressed him through breathless gasps.

"Please, take me with you," she begged. "I don't have anywhere to go."

"You're in danger here," Trent said. He was angry the woman had returned. "I had hoped you would ride back to your home."

"I have no home," the woman said. "I am alone, and I am with child."

"Well, that is not my concern," Trent said, spurring Eagle forward and cantering away. "I'm with a group of cowboys, and we're on a cattle drive. What good would you be? Besides, it's not safe. Go back to where you came from."

The woman followed close at his heels.

"I know I am a stranger, but I am throwing myself at your mercy. My husband was attacked and killed by brigands, and I have lost everything."

"Those men who attacked us, are they the brigands you speak of?" Trent asked.

"Yes… and you killed one or two, but the rest are out there, and they will come after me," the woman replied. "They threatened to kill me. Please believe me. I need to be in a safe place… for my baby."

Trent couldn't see how advanced the woman's pregnancy was, or if she was even in the delicate condition that she claimed she was in, but he decided he needed to catch up with Stan and the cowboys or risk Stan's wrath for losing sight of his twenty-five head of cattle.

As if reading his thoughts, the woman asked. "You said you're on a cattle drive. Where are the cattle?"

"Didn't you see them?" Trent asked irritably. "I had to take on our attackers while the rest of the men herded the cattle away. And now I've fallen so far back that I can barely see the lanterns bobbing in the darkness."

"I can see something, though," the woman said. "Look ahead, I can see them."

Trent galloped faster now, and to his annoyance, the woman chased after him. He could now see the lanterns again, after she had pointed them out to him.

"Alright," Trent said, feeling like he owed her for her help. "You can come with us until we find a place where we can leave you. Somewhere where you can be relatively safe and maybe find employment."

"Such places don't exist in these parts, you know," the woman replied. "Let me come with you wherever you're headed, and I'll be of help to you."

"We'll see," Trent retorted, riding faster.

Chapter Eight

"Luke Grey," Stan snarled when they approached him. "I told you I wanted none of your heroics. Why did you go back for that woman?"

Trent glared at Stan. "I didn't," he said shortly. "She came after me while I was trying to catch up with you lot after fighting off those men who attacked us."

"What's the woman's name?" Stan asked.

Trent shrugged. "I have no idea," he replied. "And no interest in knowing. She said she was with child and had nowhere to go, and she said she would be of help if we took her with us. She does have good eyesight, I'll give her that."

"The boss won't like this, you know," Stan declared.

"I didn't ask for this to happen, Stan," Trent said, keeping his voice down with an effort.

"While you were busy on your rescue, someone had to take care of the cattle assigned to you to look after," Stan said, as if looking for reasons to berate Trent.

"For the last time, Stan, I did not go after the woman. She came after me," Trent replied. "And now that she's here, maybe she can help cook the meals or something. We still have a way to travel, don't we?"

"A pregnant woman," Stan snorted. "What will you pick up next, Luke?"

Trent said nothing.

Later, they stopped for breakfast by a lake and the men had scattered to relax. Some of them were taking a dip in the lake while the cattle drank from it and cropped the grass on the banks.

Trent sat by himself, tin mug in hand, and sipped his coffee. He saw the woman go off by herself, and hoped the men would respect her privacy. In the daylight he inspected her. Her belly did not seem too large, and he was glad to see that. It would seem dangerous for her to ride in her condition.

He sat quietly as the woman approached him, coming back out of the woods. "My name's Annie," the woman said, sitting down on a rock opposite Trent.

Trent simply nodded, and continued to sip his coffee. He did not want to encourage her.

"I understand you're eager not to appear to be too familiar with me," Annie said, "but being civil shouldn't be so hard, should it?" Annie sighed and got up, returning moments later with two plates of food. She extended one to him.

"I didn't ask for that," Trent said, though he was hungry.

"No, you didn't," Annie said. "But I got it for you anyway."

"Look, Annie, I understand you feel alone, and I'm rightly sad for you. But I have a job to do, and this is a dangerous ride you're on," Trent said, giving her a cold stare. "You're here now. Just keep to your side of the fence, and I'll keep to mine, alright?"

Annie looked down at the plate she was holding out to him and shrugged. "I didn't realize there were fences involved," she said. "But so be it."

She looked firmly at him. "However, I have no friends right now, and you saved me. I feel obligated to you. And I also feel like I can trust you. Please, would you at least tell me your name?"

"Luke," Trent said, the false name coming out with difficulty. "Luke Grey."

Annie sat down with a plate of food on either side of her. Suddenly, she smiled and touched her belly.

"You might be wondering how far gone I am," Annie remarked.

"No," Trent lied. "I'm not."

"Well, I'm in my third month," Annie declared. "So this baby is coming out in just six more months. I'd like to be settled in a place well before then."

Trent felt a tightening in his gut. This didn't augur well.

"Well, you need to find someplace to have your baby, in that case," he said.

"Perhaps you could put in a good word for me at the ranch where you work," Annie said hopefully.

"You can't work while you're looking after a young 'un," Trent said gruffly. He did not think the ranch, with its illegal activities going on, was a good place for her.

"I have to," Annie said. "To survive."

Trent got up, glad when they were on their way again and he only had the cattle to worry about. But somewhere along the line, he found himself glancing anxiously at Annie. He was hoping she would soon find a safe place to deliver her child, and maybe even someone to be a father to it.

"When I get married and have a baby, Trent, would you be its Godfather?" Trent heard Ellie's voice echo.

"What does a Godfather need to do?" Trent asked.

"Just be there for the child, I guess," Ellie had smiled. "And protect him... or her."

"Well, then, I'll be there for your baby, when you have it," Trent had replied.

"Not just when it's a baby, Trent, but right through its life for as long as you live," Ellie said.

"For as long as I'm alive to take care of him or her... and you, Ellie," Trent had declared.

It seemed a lifetime away, Trent thought to himself as he pushed the cattle forward and kept his eyes peeled for brigands.

"How much longer till we get to our destination?" someone asked Stan.

"You'll know when we get there," Stan retorted. "Now keep going!"

"He's a harsh one," Annie remarked.

"This is a harsh life," Trent replied.

Annie said nothing. She was struggling to keep up.

"Are you alright?" Trent asked.

"Yes," Annie replied. "I'm just a bit tired."

"I knew she'd be a liability," Stan remarked, talking of Annie as if she wasn't right there.

Trent was silent. He was squinting into the distance.

"Stan," he said, pulling his bandana up over his face. "I sense trouble."

Stan swore under his breath and rounded up the cowboys, barking out orders and giving them a strategy to follow.

"Something's not quite right," Trent murmured under his breath.

"Listen up!" Stan barked. "We're changing direction."

"What!" Trent exclaimed, despite himself. "And how many days will that add to our journey?"

"Just a couple," Stan said hesitantly.

"What's up ahead?" one of the men queried.

"Could be cattle thieves," Stan replied. "Or could just be a pack of men going about their business." He cleared his throat. "Either way, I don't think we should engage in any kind of a fight with them. I'd far rather we take a different route and get to the market without any further fights along the way."

"Really?" one of the cowboys retorted aggressively. "Is that what you consider a solution?"

"Yes," Stan said. "It's the best I can think of."

"Well, you know what, Stan? We're not going to listen to you," the cowboy shot back. "We will stay right here, or go forward and take what comes."

Stan adjusted his hat and spat into the dirt, turning his horse as he did so, until he was facing in a different direction.

"We're going that way, you hear?" he snarled.

"Stan, with all due respect, the more we argue amongst ourselves, the closer we are to being attacked," Trent ventured.

"You shut your mouth, Luke Grey," Stan said. "When I want your opinion, I'll ask for it. Right now, you remember your place and listen to me."

Trent felt a sudden surge of anger, probably brought on by almost four days on the trail, a deficient diet and his encounter with Sandy. He glowered at Stan.

"This one time, Stan, though you may be in charge and all, I refuse to listen. I'm going forward and will take on whatever trouble lies ahead, just as long as we can get to our destination as fast as possible and return to Rock Creek ranch."

"And what if I vow to lose you on the way, Luke? Who the hell are you anyway, to try to take control of things? I'm in charge, you hear?" Stan yelled.

"I'm sorry, Stan," Trent said. "That lot ahead of us are coming closer. We need to keep the cattle safe… and all of us as well. Call it taking initiative, but I'm doing things my way right now."

"I'm with Luke!" the man who had threatened a mutiny declared.

In seconds, cries of *I'm with Luke!* went up, and turned into a war cry as Trent quickly organized five of the cowboys, and Annie, to stay with the cattle. The rest of them were going to ride up to meet the group of people coming towards them.

"You'll be sorry you mutinied, Luke!" Stan yelled.

"I'd rather fight than run, Stan!" Trent shouted back.

Trent rode before the rest of the cowboys, bandana firmly across his face and his eyes hard. He didn't care if he lived or died. At that moment, all he wanted was to reach their destination without any further delay. He was tired of running, and he was ready to shoot his anger out on someone.

Whipping out both pistols, Trent opened fire into the air to warn the men ahead of them that they meant business.

"Your cattle or your lives!" Trent heard a man cry. With a snarl, he took careful aim and began to shoot, glancing at his companions and seeing that they had fearlessly followed suit.

But Trent, in his eagerness to get the expedition over and done with, had miscalculated the ability of the men he was riding with. He soon saw that they were struggling to fight against the more seasoned band of thieves, and he found himself defending his men while fighting off their attackers.

"Luke! Watch out!" he heard someone shout a warning, and ducked just in time as one of the thieves came at him with a knife.

Trent rose up in the stirrups and caught the man's hand, turning the knife around to his own throat. He saw blood spurt and the man fall to the ground, and then stopped and stared. From around the bend, more men appeared, charging towards Trent and the band of cowboys.

In a flash, he realized that Stan had probably been right, and that the best course of action would have been to take on a few extra days of travel, in order to spare themselves the risk of combat.

As Trent and the cowboys began to fire, they saw to their surprise that the new arrivals had taken on the thieves and put them to flight. Trent bristled, remembering that Sandy Granger had said he was following them. It was strange, the way they had appeared out of nowhere and taken on the thieves. And just like that, as the thieves scattered and galloped away, the men disappeared.

"What just happened, Luke?" one of the men asked Trent.

Trent shrugged. "I don't know, but at least we can keep going, now that the trail's clear."

"Maybe. But for how long?" someone else said.

"Don't consider yourself a hero," Stan taunted Trent as they returned, "because you're not. You just mutinied and took matters into your own hands, and I'll see that you pay for it, Luke Grey."

"At least Luke took charge," Mark said, suddenly emboldened. "And he fought off the thieves so that we can keep going, rather than adding more days on the trail."

"Shut your mouth, Mark," Stan snarled. "I didn't see you fighting. Oh no, you were hiding out here, pretending to tend the cattle."

"Which I was doing," Mark replied. "And you're nobody to tell me when to talk and when not to, Stan. As of now, I vote for Luke Grey to lead us."

As a chorus went up, voting for Trent to lead them, Stan ranted on.

"You're all making a huge mistake! Luke knows nothing about the trail, and even less about this operation. You'll be sorry when the boss finds out that we failed in our mission."

"What is this mission, Stan?" Trent asked suddenly. "It's to get the cattle to the market, right? We'll get them there. Or is there something else we don't know about? Some less than legal activity that you are engaged in?"

"Hold your tongue, or you'll be sorry, Luke," Stan roared.

Trent began to round up the men and drive the cattle forward. "I'm not going to hold my tongue, Stan," he yelled back. "You're not going to intimidate any of us anymore. We are all taking charge together."

"You don't know what you're doing!" Stan stormed. "And you're going to get us all into trouble with the boss! Men, don't be fools! Don't listen to this man; he's misguiding you!"

"We choose Luke!" the cry went up. "We choose Luke!"

Trent ignored Stan and urged on the cowboys, and drove his cattle forward. The cowboys followed suit, and soon they were making faster progress along the trail. Trent was eager to hurry, wondering all the while where Sandy Granger and his men had disappeared to, and acutely aware that they may reappear at any time.

"You're quite fearless," Annie remarked admiringly, riding alongside Trent. He had slowed the group a bit, to give the horses a rest.

"Not really," Trent replied. "I suppose I don't really care whether I live or I die anymore."

"What happened to you, Luke? Disappointed in love?"

Trent replied with a derisive snort. "Love? Love has no place in my life, Annie."

"And why is that?" Annie asked, her nose wrinkled in confusion.

"Perhaps because I don't have the time for such frivolity. I have more important things on my mind. Like getting back to Rock Creek ranch in one piece."

"And I suppose I have added to your responsibilities, haven't I?" Annie remarked.

"You're your own responsibility," Trent said roughly. "You forced yourself on us, and now here you are. But that doesn't mean you're my ward or my charge. Far from it."

Annie bit her lip. "I shouldn't have presumed that I was," she said. "And I'm sorry."

Trent felt a stab of regret at being so harsh with a woman who was so obviously lonely, but he bit back his emotion. Instead, his eyes grew harder as he thought of Sandy Granger and wondered what game he was playing.

Chapter Nine

Kate was in the paddock riding one of the mustangs that Trent had broken in when Kirk Cranston came up to the gate and looked at his daughter.

"I don't know why you can't sit down with your Ma and do some needlepoint, Kate," he said.

"Maybe because it doesn't interest me as much as riding does, Pa," Kate replied cheekily.

Kirk Cranston opened his mouth to respond when he stopped, his eyes narrowing as he looked into the distance.

"Oh my!" Kate said excitedly. "The cowboys are back from the cattle drive. Now Luke Grey can…"

"Go inside, Kate," Kirk Cranston said firmly. "And stop making eyes at the ranch hands, it's not appropriate. Besides, you have to get ready. We're having the Grants to supper."

"I don't like them," Kate said, disappointed.

"Well, you'd better learn how to," Kirk said. "Clive Grant has expressed a desire to get to know you better."

"And maybe I don't want to know him any more than I do, Pa," Kate declared. "I think I know enough, and what I know does not impress me."

Kirk, however, had already rushed away, leaving his daughter grumpy and unhappy.

"Why are you having the Grants over to supper?" Kate cried, confronting her mother as she rushed into the house. "I don't want to know Clive Grant better. He is a foolish and petty man, and I have no interest in him whatsoever!"

Vanessa Cranston put a hand to her forehead. She was a frail woman of a nervous disposition, and her hands trembled as she reacted to her daughter's outburst.

"You'll have to stop rushing in on me like that, Kate," she said. "And stop behaving like a petulant child. You're a young woman now, and you need to start thinking responsibly and doing things for the welfare of the family."

"I don't know what you could possibly mean by that, Ma," Kate retorted. "The welfare of the family? We, the Cranstons, are rich… and we own one of the largest ranches in White Water. I don't need to do anything for the welfare of this family, because we have whatever we need!"

"So you think, child. Open your eyes… and your ears… and perhaps you'll realize that everything is not as it seems. So, for your own good, and to keep those pretty clothes on your back, give Clive Grant an opportunity to prove to you that he is good husband material."

"*Husband material*?" Kate cried, aghast. "You and Pa are trying to marry me off? Well, here's news for you. I'm not going to marry anybody I don't love. And right now, I'm in love with someone, and that someone is not Clive Grant."

"You're doing it again, Kate," Vanessa Cranston said, shaking her head. "You're making a fool of yourself over the new ranch hand, aren't you? I thought you'd have learned after the last experience."

Kate flushed. "That was a silly crush. I was a child then. But this is different."

"You barely know the man, Kate," Vanessa said impatiently.

"I will get to know him better," Kate replied. "I know I haven't known him very long, but I know how I feel."

"And does he reciprocate your feelings?" Vanessa queried.

"He will," Kate said firmly.

"Well, Kate," her mother declared, "since the man you claim to love is totally inappropriate as a choice of suitor, you will need to fall out of love with him quickly and set your sights on someone more… suitable."

"You want me to marry for money, Ma?" Kate asked, her lip curling with disdain.

Vanessa nodded. "Precisely, child. It's what is required. And it is what will ensure that you can keep living this life you have become so accustomed to."

"I can live rough," Kate shot back. "And a ranch hand doesn't always have to remain a ranch hand. Luke Grey is a good man and a capable one. He won't remain a ranch hand forever."

"Be dressed and ready when the Grants come, Kate," Vanessa said firmly.

***

"Who's the woman, Luke?" Kirk Cranston asked, his face red. "I hope you men haven't been doing anything you shouldn't on the trail. The woman's in a delicate state, as well."

"We rescued her from a band of thieves," Trent replied.

"We?" Stan snarled. "*You* rescued her, Luke. Just you."

"Well, yes. I saved the woman from her captors, Mister Cranston, sir," Trent replied.

"And then she came back after him, and he didn't drive her away," Stan added.

Luke nodded. "That's true. I couldn't leave her there alone. Her husband had been killed by brigands."

"Where do you propose keeping her, Luke? In your private cabin?" Kirk asked, clearly annoyed.

"No, sir," Trent replied. "I was hoping she could find some work here. She's willing to work."

"I'm sorry for imposing on you, sir," Annie cut in. "And this is not Luke Grey's fault. He acted out of kindness, and I forced him to take me along with the men so that I could feel safe. I am willing to work here. I have a great deal of homemaking skills."

Kirk Cranston replied with a derisive snort. "What can a woman do that I could need?"

"I'm a strong woman, sir. I can cook, and I've been told I make a lovely pie," Annie replied.

As the word pie, many of the men perked up.

"Well," Mr. Cranston said, "I suppose we could use some help with the meals around here…"

Chapter Ten

"You brought back a woman, Luke? How could you?" Kate cried.

"I don't understand what you mean, Kate," Trent replied.

"I heard from Pa that you picked up a woman on the trail and brought her back with you," Kate retorted.

"Not *picked up*, Kate," Trent answered, "but rescued. She was on her own and had been taken captive by some thieves. She cried out for help, and I went to her aid and told her to run. She ran back to us because she was afraid of being alone. She's pregnant. Her husband was killed. Now, if you were a sympathetic person, Kate, you would talk to your father about employing her. Maybe you could give her a job as your maid or cook, anything."

"Why do you care so much about her?" Kate asked in a half-teasing tone.

"I think you're reading too much into my intentions here, Kate. You are also, I think, making assumptions about me in relation to you," Trent ventured warily.

"What are you saying, Luke?" Kate murmured, flushing. She had not expected this reaction to her joking.

"The way you asked about Annie, the woman whom I rescued and brought here. You sounded like I'm not supposed to associate with any other woman," Trent said.

Kate flushed again. "I suppose I just felt like we were becoming… close, you know?" she faltered.

"You're my employer's daughter, Kate, therefore I treat you with respect and strive to do your bidding," Trent replied. "But you have to know that I have no place in my life for anything frivolous. No place in my life at all for anything that would take my attention away from the road."

Kate thrust her chin out. "I'll have you know that we had the Grants over to supper last night," she said. "And their son Clive Grant seems keen on me."

"That's good," Trent said. "You should consider the suit of someone so deserving of your attentions."

Kate's lower lip trembled, her façade breaking down. "But I don't want to, Luke. I want you."

"You don't really want me, Kate," Trent said, more gently this time. "You may be drawn to the idea of me. The cowboy who appears out of nowhere and breaks in a mustang or two. But I'm not who you think I am. So please, Kate, for your sake and for mine too, don't imagine that you feel anything for me."

"I'm not imagining that I have feelings for you, Luke. I do," Kate whispered.

Trent glanced up at the window where Vanessa was watching them.

"Your Ma is watching us, Kate. Go inside now," Trent urged.

Kate cast a defiant look at her mother and turned back to Trent. And before he could react, she had thrown herself into his arms and pressed her lips to his.

Trent pushed her roughly away and drew the back of his hand across his lips.

"What do you think you're doing, Kate?" he queried, distressed. He was tired of women throwing kisses at him in this way. It did not seem to end well.

"Why are you so afraid to show your feelings for me, Luke?" Kate asked.

"Because there are none to show, Kate," Luke retorted. "And you've probably lost me my job by doing what you did just now."

"Are you in love with the woman you brought back with you?" Kate demanded.

"For the last time, Kate," Trent said. "I am not in love with anyone. I have no time for such frivolity. To me, it's an unnecessary waste of time. So please, leave me to get on with more important things."

"I thought I was important," Kate huffed.

"To Clive Grant, or other similar suitors, perhaps," Trent said. "But not to me. To me, you're the boss's daughter, and I'm here to serve."

"What if I got your new friend a job as my maid?" Kate asked.

Trent sighed impatiently. "Really, Kate," he said, "can't you just be kind to this woman without expecting something in return from me? Don't you realize you're not doing me a favor by giving Annie a way to earn her keep? Do it for yourself. Because you're a good person. Don't do it because you think that will change my intentions towards you."

"I will employ her," Kate said. "And one day you will love me, Luke."

"What have you got against Clive Grant?" Trent asked, teasing her back now.

"Nothing. Except the fact that I'm to marry him as a service to my family. He's very rich, you see," Kate said.

"So is your father," Trent replied.

"Apparently my parents need me to marry for money," Kate said. "My Ma sounded like it was urgently required."

"And after your Ma saw you kiss me just now, she will rush the process," Trent said drily.

"And I will run away," Kate declared dramatically. "With you."

Trent walked back to his cabin deep in thought, beset by disturbing memories of the cattle drive.

They had pushed on with him leading the way to the market, but when they got to their destination, Trent could see that there was something not quite right.

"Move over, Luke," Stan said. "I need to handle this myself."

"What's to handle?" one of the cowboys sneered. "We know how to sell cattle."

"Ready to do business?" a man asked, coming up to Stan.

Stan nodded. "Yes, sir," he said, tipping his hat to the man.

"Well, come this way," the man said. "Are these from Rock Creek Ranch?"

"Yes," Stan replied, glaring at Trent as his eyes widened.

"They're in good shape, considering the distance," the man remarked.

The cowboys herded the cattle into the enclosure the man pointed out to them, and then stood by their horses, undecided about what they should do next.

"I need to eat something," Annie said. She looked pale and weak, and Trent was concerned.

"There doesn't seem to be any place selling food here," Trent remarked.

"Days without any bread or biscuits has left me feeling pretty undernourished myself," Mark declared. "I'll go and look for some food and provisions."

"I'll come too," Trent said.

"So will I," Saul, the cook, chimed in.

"I see a mercantile," Mark remarked.

"Let's go and buy some flour and maybe even some meat," Saul replied.

"I guess I'll leave you both to it," Trent murmured, observing Stan and the buyer walking together, deep in conversation. On an impulse, he decided to follow them.

Trent was ducking into a tiny lane, to escape being spied by Stan and the buyer, when he heard a familiar voice and blanched.

"Sandy Granger," he growled. "What are you doing here?"

"Same as you," Sandy said. "I'm following your friend Stan, and the rest of you actually."

Trent glared at Sandy. "Look, stop acting like you're on my side. I will get to the bottom of whatever it is that you're up to, and I will avenge Ellie's death," he said.

"Believe me, I also want to find Ellie's murderer," Sandy replied.

"Look in the mirror and you will," Trent snarled. "My hands are tied right now, but the moment I can, I will take you down, Sandy Granger."

"You're blinded by anger, Trent," Sandy said. "But when the mists clear, you will see that you need me on your side."

Trent didn't respond. He could hear voices, and one sounded familiar. He peered down the alley to see who it was.

"But these cattle have a different mark on them," the buyer was saying. *"Are you sure they're from Rock Creek Ranch?"*

"Why would I lie to you?" Stan replied. *"The boss has different branding irons for different herds. He has so many that he has developed this system to keep a better count of them."*

"I don't believe you," the buyer said. *"These have been stolen!"*

"No," Stan protested.

"I could have you arrested right away," the buyer declared.

"We had a deal, and I'd thank you to keep it," Stan said.

"I told you before, I don't do business with thieves," the buyer shot back.

"I could cut you a deal," Stan said, trying to mollify the buyer. *"I'll bring the price down a bit. We're tired. We need to get back."*

"Two for the price of one, or there's no deal," the buyer said.

Trent had seen enough and backed away, turning to head towards the rest of the men.

"You still here?" he said to Sandy, who was still standing exactly where he had left him.

"I've heard enough, actually," Sandy replied. "I'm going now. I'll see you around, Trent Conway."

"Will you be following us back to Rock Creek Ranch?" Trent asked.

"I'll be around if you need me, Trent," Sandy answered.

Trent had watched Sandy leave, his gun hand twitching. He was still reconsidering his decision to wait Sandy out. And then he stood still as he heard sounds of a scuffle on the other side of the alley. It was Stan and the buyer again.

Trent looked into the alley just in time to see Stan with his arm looped around the buyer's neck. He was pressing down on his throat so that his eyes bulged and holding a gun to his head.

"Give me the money you owe me!" Stan yelled.

"What if I don't? You going to drive your stolen cattle all the way back to Rock Creek Ranch and that no-good boss of yours?" the buyer taunted.

"If you don't pay me, I'll blow your brains out and take them to your wife!" Stan roared.

"I don't buy stolen cattle," the man protested. "I don't want the real owners coming after me."

Trent froze as a shot rang out, and then the buyer slumped to the ground, blood oozing from a wound in his head. Stan began rifling through his pockets and pulling out wads of notes.

"What are you staring at, Luke?" Stan growled. He had seen Trent in the shadows, watching. "Get back to the men and wait for me, you hear?"

"You got it, boss," Trent replied. He knew Stan was ruthless, but he hadn't realized how much. "So, he's dead, then?"

"Scum deserved to die," Stan said, without a trace of emotion. "That's what happens to people who cross me, Luke. Be warned."

"Luke Grey?" a woman's voice addressed him as he reached his cabin.

"Missus Cranston, ma'am, what can I do for you?" Trent said, tipping his hat. He surprised by his visitor.

"I'm sorry for intruding," Vanessa said, "but I feel I must speak to you, before it's too late."

"May I invite you inside?" Trent asked politely.

"No, thank you," Vanessa replied. "I will only take a minute of your time."

"Sure then. Well, ma'am, please tell me how I may be of assistance," Trent said. He was aware that Vanessa had seen Kate kiss him only minutes earlier.

"Please, don't get involved with my daughter," Vanessa said flatly, looking him in the eye.

"I'm not involved," Trent declared.

"Maybe not yet," Vanessa said. "But Kate always gets her way. You are her way out of a marriage of convenience, and she will use you to escape what she needs to do for her family."

"With all due respect, ma'am," Trent said. "I don't think this is any of my business."

"It is indeed your business, Luke Grey. Or should I say, Trent Conway?" Vanessa answered, surveying Trent through narrowed eyes.

Trent swallowed several times and wondered why he hadn't already taken off. He'd been getting some bad feelings about the ranch, and Sandy showing up was sure a bad sign.

"I checked up on you, you know, when I noticed Kate's fascination with you," Vanessa said.

."I don't know what to say," Trent held his hands up, "except that I mean no harm. I'm here to earn a livelihood."

"Under a false name?" Vanessa said coldly. "Using my sources, I learned that you're on the run. And for murder, no less."

"I was framed, ma'am," Trent replied, though he feared words now were useless. "I didn't kill anyone."

"You have a violent nature, I'm told," Vanessa replied. "I heard about the killings on the trail."

"Those were for our protection," Trent answered. "I was doing my job."

"And perhaps you were also doing your job by killing that poor girl that we heard about," Vanessa said.

"She was a dear friend, a sister to me," Trent said. "I did not kill her, but I am trying to find out who did. But I am having to search in secret." He hoped sharing some degree of the truth would help soothe the woman.

"Well, I do know you are a criminal. I know where you and my husband got those cattle," Vanessa said. "So don't play innocent with me, young man. I know you've killed. What I can say is, leave my daughter alone. I'd far rather she marries rich and brings this family the money it needs. This cattle ranching folly is not a good plan for the future. And particular how my husband carries it out—and the men it attracts. It is a pursuit that will one day catch up with us and cause untold trouble."

"I have no interest in your daughter, ma'am," Trent said firmly.

"That's what they all say," Vanessa declared. "But I know your secret, Trent Conway, and I will tell everyone who you are and what you did if you encourage Kate any further."

"You have nothing to worry about," Trent said, tipping his hat. Yes, it was surely time to go.

After Vanessa left, Trent hurried into his cabin and threw his meager belongings into his saddlebag. Then he fetched Eagle and mounted quickly.

"Hey!" Stan called, as he trotted past him. "Where are you off to?"

"The saloon in town," Trent said, not stopping.

A figure on a horse stepped out into his path, and Trent drew Eagle up so suddenly that he was almost thrown from the saddle.

"What the hell are you doing?" Trent cried, as Annie put up a hand to halt him.

"Luke," Annie said, "take me with you."

"Where to?" Trent asked. "What are you talking about?"

"I overheard Missus Cranston talking to her daughter and telling her about you. Who you are…" Annie said. "And I guess that's why you have your saddlebag and are riding away. So please, take me with you."

"Annie, that is just not possible," Trent said, moving Eagle around her and preparing to move forward. "I cannot take a woman where I am going."

"I can't stay here, Luke, or whatever your name is. I don't trust these people," Annie said, urging her horse to match Trent's pace. They trotted down the road.

"Annie," Trent replied. "You have a good job and a place to live. So stay here and work for now. Have your baby and take care of it, until it gets old enough for you to leave on your own. I can't take you with me."

"You know I can help you!" Annie said. "And we don't have to go far. Maybe just a few towns away. Away from this family!" Her voice had grown louder as she made her case.

"Hush, woman! You'll bring out the household and have us caught," Trent said. "Now be sensible and go back."

"I can't," Annie said. "It's not safe."

"Look, Annie," Luke pleaded, "I'm on the run. It's not safe for you to even be with me. Who knows what Kirk Cranston will do when he hears I've fled the scene?" He realized he was tempted to allow her to accompany him, at least for a few days. He would be less conspicuous traveling with a woman, and could still drop her off in a safe town some miles away.

"They just wanted you to leave because of Kate developing feelings for you," Annie said suddenly, still trotting slowly alongside him.

"Wait, what's that?" Trent queried, slowing down.

"Kate developing feelings for you," Annie repeated.

"Not that," Trent said, cocking his ear to listen. "That! I hear horses."

"Luke, there's a someone riding up after us," Annie said, slowing her horse to glance over her shoulder.

He felt the blood run cold in his veins. He had a bad feeling about this, and wanted to get ahead of the pursuer so Annie could slip off the road and out of sight. He did not want her exposed to any violence.

"Don't stop and don't look back," Trent instructed her sharply.

Trent urged Eagle to gallop faster. Annie's horse quickly sped up to keep pace. He was reluctant to enter into a gunfight here, but aware that there may be no escaping one.

"Keep going!" he shouted to Annie, slowing his horse in the road after they had gotten ahead of the man. "I'll deal with whoever it is."

"But we don't even know what he wants," she protested.

"Just go, and get out of sight, at least."

She started to speak again, but then the man came into clear view. Trent was surprised to recognize him.

"Stop right there, Luke Grey!" Stan yelled, drawing closer as Trent slowed down.

"What's wrong, Stan? Why are you chasing us?" Trent asked.

"The boss sent me after you. Your secret is out."

"My secret?" Trent queried. "I don't know what you mean, Stan."

"You're not who you say you are," Stan said, his eyes on Trent's hands. His own also stayed near his holster. "And you're a murderer."

"*You're* a murderer, Stan, not me," Trent declared. "You killed the buyer we met at the cattle market. And you stole all his money."

"I took the payment for the cattle," Stan retorted. "I never stole anything."

"You led us all into that huge cattle heist, Stan," Trent said, drawing his pistols.

"I wouldn't try any funny business, Luke… or whatever your real name is," Stan said.

"Yes, I wouldn't, Luke. Or should I say, Trent Conway," Kirk Cranston said, riding up. "Where are you off to? And why did you run when you saw we were after you?" Kirk asked coldly.

Trent shrugged. "I guess I'm just ready for a change of scenery. Maybe some of the recent events on the trail made me jumpy, too."

"Well, now you're coming back to Rock Creek Ranch," Kirk Cranston said. "I know who you are, and I will turn you in if you refuse to do as I say."

"Turn me in for what? I haven't done anything wrong," Trent shot back.

"You would say that, wouldn't you? However, even if you are innocent of the crime you are being hunted down for, the fact is, you're being hunted down, and you took refuge in Rock Creek. You also, I heard, took over from Stan here when he was about to make some bad choices along the trail. And I heard you killed men in cold blood, when the need arose. I need someone like you. Or, I can offer you a different choice…" Kirk said.

"Which is …?" Trent queried, sure he knew the response.

"Be arrested and taken behind bars, for a crime you have already been convicted of," Kirk drawled.

"Are you blackmailing me?" Trent asked.

"Call it what you like," Kirk said.

"I will come back, on one condition," Trent said.

"You don't get to lay down any conditions, Trent Conway," Kirk retorted.

"A request then," Trent said. "Please re-employ Annie. She needs the work and a place to have her baby."

Trent frowned, then, as he saw another horseman riding up. He stiffened as he realized who it was.

"What's going on here, Mister Cranston?" Sandy Granger asked.

"Nothing that I haven't already put a stop to, Clive," Kirk replied.

"Clive?" Trent repeated, his eyebrows going up.

"Yes, this is Clive Grant," Kirk said, "the son of my good friend, Philip Grant. And soon to be my daughter's betrothed."

Trent blinked. So Sandy Granger was now Clive Grant?

Annie had gone ahead as Trent had asked her, but now returned to where Trent stood, confronted by Kirk Cranston, Stan Long, and the man who used to be known to Trent as Sandy Granger.

"Luke," Annie said, clutching her belly, "something is happening. Something feels wrong. I think you were right, about being ready."

"Well," Kirk Cranston said, guffawing. "This situation does get more interesting, doesn't it?"

"All that riding on the trail, and then now, trying to run away. I guess it has its consequences," Stan remarked with a cruel laugh. "Come on, Trent, take care of your woman."

Trent, however, caught a different meaning. He had not mentioned 'being ready,' so what was she referring to?

Annie slid off her horse and stood carefully on the ground, not far from where Kirk Cranston and the others were standing. Trent turned to her and met her eyes briefly, reading the message in them. His hands went to his pistols, just as Annie let out a cry of pain and bent over.

As she did, she caught Kirk Cranston's ankles, and before he could react, had toppled him to the ground. Stan lunged forward to help his boss, and Trent took advantage of the man's distraction to sink a bullet into the back of his head and one into Kirk Cranston's chest. The sound of swiftly retreating hoofbeats caught his ear, and Trent looked to see that Sandy—or Clive Grant— was galloping away.

He took aim and fired both pistols, but the man was too far away, and the bullets didn't meet their target.

"Luke! Watch out!" Annie cried as Stan sat up and aimed his pistol at Trent. Trent spun, sinking two bullets into Stan's chest, and watched him fall lifeless against Kirk.

"Is he alive?" Annie asked, pointing to Kirk.

Trent leaned over to check if Kirk was breathing. Suddenly, Kirk reached out and grabbed Luke's throat. The grip was weak, as the man was mortally wounded. And then, all at once, he heard

a loud thunk. He felt Kirk Cranston let go and fall
back.

"What…?" He saw then that Annie had
struck Kirk a blow on his head with a heavy rock.
So, he smiled, she could handle herself. And that
trick with the baby coming had been quite brilliant.

"Luke!" Annie cried. He came out of his
thoughts and looked out to where a host of
horsemen were coming at them. They were still far
over the other hill, but they needed to get moving.

"Sandy," Trent muttered. "He must have
brought them. Let's go," he said to Annie, helping
her onto her horse and leaping onto Eagle.

Together, they rode quickly, covering the
miles and not looking back. They wove their way
through woods to hide their tracks and slept in the
thicket that night. Finally, Trent was convinced
the danger had passed, and their pursuers had
given up.

Chapter Eleven

"If I could just find my way back to my home town, that would be perfect," Annie said.

"Well, I could take you there, and then be on my way," Trent replied.

"I would be so grateful," Annie said, smiling. "You could stay as long as you like, too. The least I can do is offer you a roof over your head until you decide what you want to do next, Luke." Her voice faltered as she said his fake name. He knew it now sounded strange in her mouth.

"There's something I have to tell you, Annie," Trent said. "I'm not Luke Grey. That is not my name."

"Oh?" Annie queried, glad he had decided to bring it up. "Who are you, then?"

"Trent Conway is my name, and I have been on the run for a murder I didn't commit. I thought I knew who the actual murderer was, and now I don't know if my suspicions were correct."

"So we'll find him, the murderer. We could work together," Annie said.

He shook his head. "You also need to know something else. There is no *we*, Annie. I saved your life, and that's it. I go my way, once I get you to your home town, and you go your way. Is that understood?"

Annie bit her lip as she nodded. "I understand," she said. "So, you are not looking for help, or a partner?"

"No," Trent growled. "I am a fugitive, and a man on the run doesn't have time for things like that. Especially now when I will also be wanted for the killing of Kirk Cranston and Stan Long. But I was brought up to do the right thing, Annie, and the right thing, at this moment, is to take you safely home."

"And what about you?" Annie asked.

"I'm a fugitive. I'll keep doing what a fugitive does: run," Trent replied.

***

Together, they headed out onto the trail. Trent knew that once he returned Annie to her home, he would be alone again. Now, he would be hunted for the murder of Stan Long and Kirk Cranston—and this time, the blood was on his hands.

He would have to keep running, he knew that now. But before he ran too far, he needed to find out one more thing.

Who was Sandy Granger, really?

********   *The End*   ********

Many thanks for taking the time to buy and read through this book.

It means lots to be supported by SPECIAL readers like YOU.

Hope you enjoyed the book; please support my writing by leaving an honest review to assist other readers.

With Regards,

Mike Dale